SINCERELY Sicily

SINCERELY Sicily

TAMIKA BURGESS

HARPER
An Imprint of HarperCollinsPublishers

Library of Congress Cataloging-in-Publication Data

Names: Burgess, Tamika, author.

Title: Sincerely Sicily / by Tamika Burgess.

Description: First edition. | New York, NY : Harper, [2023] | Audience: Ages 8-12. | Audience: Grades 4-6. | Summary: Sixth-grader Sicily Jordan learns to use her voice and to find joy in who she is—a Black Panamanian fashionista who rocks her braids with pride—while confronting prejudice both in the classroom and at home.

Identifiers: LCCN 2022008191 | ISBN 9780063159600 (hardcover)

Subjects: CYAC: Racially mixed people—Fiction. | Panamanian Americans— Fiction. | Self-esteem—Fiction. | Prejudices—Fiction. | Middle schools—Fiction. | Schools—Fiction. | Families—Fiction. | LCGFT: Novels.

Classification: LCC PZ7.1.B8744 Si 2023 | DDC [E]—dc23

LC record available at https://lccn.loc.gov/2022008191

Typography by Corina Lupp

22 23 24 25 26 LBC 5 4 3 2 1

First Edition

For the young Black girls who don't know it yet but will soon learn that seeing themselves represented in books matters.

ONE

Sicily Jordan

DEMANDING TO SEE the email only shows me how real this all is. Pa's phone trembles in my hands as I read it for myself. I almost can't get past the words:

SICILY JORDAN is registered and has been placed in a sixth-grade class.

It's like all of a sudden, they are the only words I've ever learned in my entire life.

My fingers grip the phone tighter and tighter as I keep reading those words over and over, hoping for them to change magically. It's because of them that Ma and Pa decided that I'm going to Shirley Chisholm instead of Ravenwood Middle School.

"Que ridículo," Abuela Belén says, as she rubs my shoulder.

1

"They can't send an email a week before school starts and expect you to change all the plans you've already made."

I stretch myself out on the couch and rest my head on Abuela's lap, closing my eyes before my tears spill over. Abuela has been spending a lot more time with us since coming back from her trip to Panamá a few months ago. Ma isn't a fan of Abuela being here so much, but I'm glad she's here at this moment—I need her.

"Sicily. Are you *really* going to cry?" My older brother, Enrique, says from where he is lying on the living room floor. "About a school?"

My eyes fly open.

"Shut up!" I shout at him.

Ma gives me that look I know all too well, the one that says, *Calm down before I calm you down.* So I quickly look back at the phone still in my hand and read the sentence one more time before forcing myself to look at the rest of the email.

Fr: Administration@Chisholm.edu
To: EnriqueJordanSR@eMail.com
Subject: Shirley Chisholm Middle School Is Open!

Hello MR. ENRIQUE JORDAN SR.,

Since the beginning of the calendar year, construction

has been diligently taking place on 15 acres of land at the corner of Broadway and 7th Street.

While it was a tight deadline, I am pleased to inform you that Shirley Chisholm Middle School will open next week, in time for the beginning of the school year. Since your address is within our new school zone, your child SICILY JORDAN is registered and has been placed in a sixth-grade class. If you have already made other arrangements for your child's schooling, please let us know as soon as possible, and we will unenroll your child.

Although we are ready to open, we are still in the process of adding to our campus. Because of this, sixth-grade classes will be held in portable classrooms, where students will stay with the same teacher for every subject.

Starting tomorrow, between 10:00 a.m. and 3:00 p.m., you and your child can visit the campus to take a tour and pick up a copy of the school handbook. Additional emails regarding school rules, dress code, and classroom assignments will be sent out in the following days.

Please do not hesitate to contact me if you have any questions.

Looking forward to a great year,
Principal Cynthia Rivas
Shirley Chisholm Middle School

At the end of fifth grade, rumors started going around about the new middle school opening in time for sixth grade. The rest of the Tether Squad—Evelyn, Samara, and Alexis—didn't worry about it because they live closer to Ravenwood Middle School and knew for sure that's where they'd be going. I wasn't as confident.

Unlike my friends, I live right on the very border of the newly drawn district zone. The fear of being separated from the Tether Squad, especially Evelyn, planted itself in the back of my mind and sat there all summer, driving me crazy whenever we passed by the campus construction site. Every time I saw it, I prayed that it wouldn't open in time for the upcoming school year. My parents were also concerned about the timing, so they enrolled me at Ravenwood, which put all my fears to rest.

Even when the school started coming together fast in July, Pa and Ma never mentioned it, so I didn't let it bother me. I knew the new school would open at some point. I figured by the time it did, I would be in seventh or eighth grade and my parents would just let me stay at Ravenwood since I'd already be there.

I should have known something would happen to mess up my plans. I'm not giving up though. I force myself to sit upright on the couch, then cough to get air circulating through my body again.

Think, Sicily, think.

I decide to go with the most obvious thing. The thing they seem to have forgotten. "We already have a plan. That's why you enrolled me at Ravenwood with everyone else."

"We enrolled you at Ravenwood because it was our *only* option at the time," Ma says. "It was going to be a huge scheduling issue for us. It's a twenty-minute drive away, and we would've had to get up very early every morning. And then Pa and I would've had to deal with traffic both ways."

"Chisholm is down the street, and now you can walk home from school," Pa says, like I've won some kind of prize. "You're always complaining, saying that we treat you like a baby. Now you get to be responsible for getting yourself back home. So this is a good thing."

Really? Walking back home is supposed to change my mind about everything? It's supposed to make me happy about going to a new school? Just as I open my mouth to say this, Abuela puts her small wrinkly hands up and motions like a referee calling a time-out.

"Espérate un momentito," she says. "Let me see this email."

Even though I'm not sure how well she reads English, I hand Abuela Pa's phone. The living room is silent as Abuela lowers her glasses and looks over the top of them to read. I stare at her slightly bent fingers as they hold the phone.

A little bit of relief falls over me as Abuela looks up from the phone and smiles. She always has my back. Abuela is the one who gets Pa to say yes to something he and Ma have already said no to me about, like when I wanted a cell phone and my parents kept saying I was too young. Once I told Abuela, it took her only an hour to get Pa to change his mind. I'm not sure how or when Ma came around to the idea. Either way, it didn't matter because Abuela always knows exactly what to say.

"Problem solved," Abuela announces as she tosses the phone to the couch. "I can take Sicily to school. That way, no one has to change their schedule or worry about traffic."

"Perfect! Thank you, Abuela." I tilt my head back and shake my fists like I'm cheering at a game.

"No, Belén, please. That's not necessary," Ma says.

"We don't want you doing all that driving, Mamá," Pa says. "Your sight is getting blurry, and your arthritis is getting worse," he says while pointing to each finger on his hand as he lists Abuela's issues.

A few months ago, Pa told Enrique and me about Abuela's arthritis and explained that the joints in her fingers are starting to swell more often, and she wouldn't be able to use her hands and fingers for long periods without being in pain. So Pa is right. The last thing Abuela should be doing is trying to grip a steering wheel for long periods every day.

Flip. Flop.

My stomach can't handle any of this. I can feel everything I ate earlier this evening tumbling around inside me, like clothes in a dryer. My parents look at me, then turn to each other. Is this it? Are they going to change their minds?

"Sicily," Ma says. And by the way she says my name—like she feels sorry for me—I know Ma won't budge.

I turn to Pa, my only hope. "Please don't make me go to a school I'll have zero friends in. It's only drop-off and pickup. I promise to never make you late." I clasp my hands and lace my fingers together so tightly that my knuckles start turning white. "I'll even do more chores around the house. I'll wash the cars, vacuum the whole house, keep my room clean. Please, just don't make me go to Chisholm." He just shakes his head from side to side.

Flip. Flop.

"Geez, drama mama," Enrique says while scrolling on his phone. "Let it go."

"Leave her alone," Ma tells him.

Enrique gets up from the floor where he'd been lying the entire time and heads toward the stairs. As he passes by me, he makes a face like the room stinks and says something to me. But I can't hear him because my ears feel clogged.

Flip. Flop.

"You don't understand what it'll be like," I say. "There isn't anybody I know who's going to Chisholm. And everyone is going to know someone else already. I'm going to be the only one without any friends."

"Sicily, plenty of students from your elementary school

7

are also going to Chisholm. You *will* know people," Ma says. "And you'll get to meet new people who come from the other three elementary schools in the area. I think you'll be fine— it's just school."

JUST SCHOOL! THIS IS SIXTH GRADE! MIDDLE SCHOOL.

Ma has lost her mind. There is no way it's *just school*. Not after the Tether Squad and I have planned out outfits for almost the entire first month. It's not *just school* when all year long we've been excited about switching classes and the possibility of all four of us having at least one together. And it's definitely not *just school* when Evelyn and I said we'd try out for Ravenwood's spring play, where she would be the star of the show and I would be behind the scenes writing the script full of the words that would cement her acting career.

"You two need to listen to what your hija is saying," Abuela says. "Give her a chance to explain herself."

Ma looks at me from the corner of her eye. She turns to Abuela and looks like she's about to say something before shaking her head and going to the kitchen. Maybe there is a little bit of hope after all. With Ma out of the room, Abuela can work her magic.

"Mamá, there's nothing for Sicily to explain," Pa says to Abuela. "The decision has been made." Pa grabs the remote, switches the TV channel to a baseball game, and then spreads out on the couch.

"Pa—" I start to say, only to snap my mouth shut. Before I can finish, Ma shouts, "Sicily! Enough!" from the kitchen, letting me know *this* conversation is over.

A loud bang unclogs my ears. It sounds like the judge has banged her gavel in *Caso Cerrado*, the TV court show Abuela watches on Telemundo. My eyes get blurry, and when I blink to clear them, tears escape and race down my cheeks.

My life is ruined. When I get up to leave, I feel like my legs aren't going to hold me up, and I'm going to crash down to the floor. Abuela stands and puts her arms around me as I stare into space. Unable to speak, I pat her back a few times, then slowly let go of her. Even though Abuela's hugs usually make things better, right now I want to be alone.

I head toward the stairs and go up to my room. After shutting my bedroom door, my phone chimes *BOING! BOING!* alerting me of texts from the Tether Squad.

Samara Smith

I found some new outfit ideas for school.

Evelyn Martin

Me too!

Alexis Brim

Send screenshots

TWO
My Fave

"GET OUT," ENRIQUE says.

"No."

After stressing about this all night, today I find myself lying on the floor in Enrique's room trying to explain to him why I don't want to switch schools, and I am beyond annoyed. He's incapable of understanding.

Picking at my neon yellow nail polish, I try to focus on all the noises I'm hearing instead: the faint music coming from the headset Enrique's wearing, tree leaves scraping against his window, and the sound of me breathing hard through my nose.

"You're being so dramatic about this whole thing," he says. Enrique's sitting in his red-and-black cushioned gamer chair in front of his TV. He's thumbing the buttons on his wireless controller so hard it sounds like it's going to crack.

"Who, me?" Enrique hasn't responded to me nor taken his eyes off the TV screen since I came into his room, so I have no idea if he's finally talking to me or the person his headset has connected him to.

"Yes, *you*."

Enrique is three years older than me. He is Pa's twin, right down to his light skin tone and the dimple on his left cheek. I guess that's why he is Enrique Jr. and Pa is Enrique Sr. The only difference between them is that Pa has a military haircut, while Enrique is letting his hair grow out. Enrique and I get along pretty well. Even though we argue, sometimes we have these cool conversations that make me think of him as a friend, not just my brother.

Right now is not one of those times.

"I am not being dramatic," I say, rolling my eyes.

"Your friends are still going to be your friends," he says. "It doesn't matter which school you go to. Besides, every school is the same thing—boring." Even though he isn't looking back at me, I know he's rolling his eyes.

"Ugh. You just don't get it," I say. I yank down on the string hanging besides Enrique's window, and the blinds fly up, letting the dimming evening sunlight fill his bedroom. "It's different for boys. You guys can just—"

"Pull that back down," he says, cutting me off.

"No, you need fresh air. It smells like feet and Fritos in here."

11

I slide his window open, press my left cheek against its frame, and stare down the street. Outside is dead. No one is riding bikes or playing basketball in their driveways, and no cars are coming down the street. I don't bother finishing what I was saying to Enrique. I know he doesn't want to hear it. My parents don't want to either. I know if I say anything else about Ravenwood, they're going to explode all over me.

I need my fave, my abuela. When I called her earlier, her phone just rang. I bet it's on silent, sitting at the bottom of her big black handbag.

BOING! BOING!

"My phone!" I take off down the hallway to my room, where my phone continues alerting me of incoming messages. I spot it on my bed, the screen lighting up as texts keep coming in. I rush over to it, closing my bedroom door behind me, but it's only the Tether Squad.

Evelyn Martin

I got my new Vans!

Now I have everything I need for my first week of school outfits.

What about you guys?

Samara Smith

Im only missing a silver pair of hoop earrings.

12

Alexis Brim

IM SO EXCITED!! I cant wait to be in sixth grade.

No more baby elementary school for us.

This time yesterday, I was just as excited as they are. Now everything has changed. And I haven't had it in me to tell them what's going on yet.

I drop backward onto my bed. Staring up at the unlit Christmas lights hanging around my ceiling, I think back to when I first met the Tether Squad. It was first grade. We became friends after Evelyn and I tied for first place in our school tetherball competition. Samara and Alexis placed second and third. Since then, we've told each other everything—no secrets, ever.

Sicily Jordan

Sorry I didnt text back earlier.

My parents are making me go to Chisholm.

Evelyn Martin

What? NOOOOOOOOOOOO!

Samara Smith

It opened??

13

Sicily Jordan

Yup. Right in time for the first day of school.

Alexis Brim

Oh no. ☹

Three bubbles pop up in the text box, letting me know one of them is typing. Then the bubbles disappear, only to quickly show up again.

Evelyn Martin

Maybe youll like it? Since its a new school. I bet they will have all new classrooms, computers, and stuff.

There go the bubbles again. I curl up on my bed like a baby, with my knees close to my chest as I watch to see who will text next. They probably have no idea what to say. None of us expected anything like this to happen.

Alexis Brim

I heard Ravenwood has old, hot classrooms that smell like the inside of a dumpster.

Sicily Jordan

> **Sicily Jordan**
>
> Im so sad I wont be with you guys.

Samara Smith

Me too. We will still hang out, text, post on each others pages. Deal?

Evelyn Martin

Deal.

Alexis Brim

Deal.

> **Sicily Jordan**
>
> Deal.

"Amor." My bedroom door slowly opens.

"Abuela!" I jump up from my bed and almost knock her down as I wrap my arms around her. I haven't been this happy to see her since she first returned from Panamá.

"I called you."

"Sí, I forgot that my phone was on silent."

I want to tell Abuela to stop doing that because she could miss an important call, like mine earlier, except she looks kind of tired. With my hands on her shoulders, I guide Abuela over to my bed so she can sit.

"How are you feeling?" I ask.

"Good." She taps my knee and smiles at me. "But I want to know how *you're* doing. I know you're not happy about this whole school thing."

"I guess I'm fine," I say. "There's nothing else I can do to change their minds, right?" I look at Abuela and give her a side smile, then cross my fingers. Hopefully, she has another idea.

"Right. When I tried to tell them I can take you to school, you heard their answer." I do my best not to let Abuela see my disappointment. "I'm sorry there's nothing I can do."

"None of this is your fault," I say to her.

I put my arm around her and rest my head on her shoulder. I could tell Abuela wasn't happy last night when Pa listed all her "issues," so I just sit with her since she needs cheering up too.

I don't have the heart to tell her to her face that my parents are right, and it really would be too much for her to have to get up early every morning and drive across town twice. I don't even like getting up early, so I definitely don't want to be the reason Abuela should have to. She deserves to sleep in or stay in bed all day and watch her novelas.

"Sicily," Ma calls from the hallway. She comes into my room holding two big reusable bags that are so full of clothes they look like they're going to pop. She gives Abuela a half smile and mouths *hello* to her.

"These are for you," Ma says, handing me the bags.

I immediately start digging through them, hoping one of them has the blue crop-top hoodie sweater I saw last week at the mall. But no. One bag is full of a bunch of gross beige-colored clothes—a pair of shorts, a skirt that looks super long, and two pairs of pants. The other bag has five white collared shirts.

"What am I supposed to do with these?" I ask, holding up one of the shirts with my index finger and thumb.

"It's your school uniform," Ma says with a huge smile on her face.

Abuela gasps and puts her hand up to her chest. "Tan feo," she says, shaking her head.

When I unfold one of the shirts, I see the words *Shirley Chisholm Middle School* stitched above the pocket on the right side.

"No one said anything about a uniform."

"We got another email this afternoon."

"Ugh. Ma," I whine.

Ma picks up one of the shirts and holds it up to me.

"You're going to look so cute. Just like me when I was your age." Although I get my thick eyebrows from Pa, my dark brown skin, button nose, and squinty eyes are all from Ma. "You know, the kids in Panamá wear school uniforms too."

I want to scream, *So what?* Only I know better. My bottom lip starts trembling, and I know tears are coming soon.

"Sicily, I know this is not what you want," Ma says. "It is what it is. I'm sorry."

Abuela reaches for my hand, and I give it to her. Even

though her thumb and pinky fingers are slightly bent, her hand is just as smooth as it always was.

"Oh, I almost forgot," Ma says. "Here's the sweater to go with your uniform." She pulls out an orange monstrosity from the bottom of one of the bags.

Ma lays the sweater out on the bed and heads to the door after telling us to come down for dinner soon.

"Sicily, look at me," Abuela says.

I let go of her hand and shift my body on my bed so I'm facing her.

"It will be okay," she says.

"No one understands, Abuela. All of my friends who I've gone to school with since first grade are going to Ravenwood." I close my eyes and continue. "I don't want to make new friends."

Abuela puts her hand on my head. Thankfully, instead of saying anything about my loose, fuzzy cornrows (like she always does), Abuela stays on topic. She pats my head and says, "There's nothing wrong with making new friends. You could join a sports team. That's an easy way to make friends and make school fun at the same time."

"I don't know about that," I say. "Sports aren't my thing."

"I remember you were excited about writing the script for a play," Abuela says. "Maybe your new school will let you do that too. Or maybe they'll have a writing club. You used to write all the time, you know, before Abuelo . . ."

Abuela pauses and looks down at the carpet. I hear her swallow hard before she continues. "Remember what Abuelo used to always say. 'Being positive when things are falling apart will change the situation for the better.'"

Abuela slides her hand into her shirt pocket. When she pulls it out, she gives me a gold anklet with a small butterfly dangling from it. I cup the anklet in my palm and close my eyes.

"I bought it a while ago. Instead of giving it to you on your birthday like I planned, I want you to wear it on your first day and remember what I said. It will all work out," Abuela says. "You hear me? I promise it will."

Just when I think no one cares about what I want or how I feel, Abuela is there for me. She always has this special way of doing the smallest thing that ends up meaning the world to me. If I'm being forced to go to this new school, at least I'll have a little something from her with me, so I won't feel completely alone.

THREE

eeee

Shirley Chisholm Middle School

I STEP THROUGH the thick gray metal school gate entrance and look from side to side. Everything is gray. Gray walls. Gray benches. Gray lunch tables. Gray ramps leading to gray portable trailer classrooms with gray doors. Even the sky is gray. This place looks exactly how I feel on the inside. No, that isn't quite right. Actually, I'm red on the inside—annoyed that I have to be here.

I don't even have Abuela's anklet as a reminder to do what Abuelo used to say: be positive. Last night, I'd laid out the anklet on my dresser next to the bracelets and earrings I'd planned to wear today. Those were still there when I woke up, yet somehow the anklet grew legs and walked away overnight.

It's already been a horrible start to my first day at

Chisholm and I haven't even walked into my classroom. I think back to my "Why I Hate My New School" list that's tucked under my pillow at home.

WHY I HATE MY NEW SCHOOL
#1 The Tether Squad isn't there
#2 No spring play with Evelyn
#3 I HAVE TO WEAR AN UGLY UNIFORM
#4 I DON'T GET TO SWITCH CLASSES FOR EACH
   SUBJECT PERIOD
#5 My anklet is missing

Be positive, I tell myself, thinking of Abuelo. So I look around and try to find at least *one* good thing about this place. Nope, I can't do it. This school is so ugly—nothing like my old elementary school. Everything was so colorful there, with bright murals painted on all the walls. Even the hand-ball courts had artwork. This looks like a jail.

Students walk past me, and even though I recognize a lot of faces from last year, I still make it my mission not to make eye contact with any of them. There's no point in trying to make friends; no one will ever be like the Tether Squad. Plus, it's weird that we're all dressed the same. I keep my head low and follow the crowd, assuming they are walking toward the courtyard, until some girl crosses right in front of me out of

21

nowhere and hands me a bright orange sheet of paper. Before I can say *Excuse you*, she's gone, lost in the sea of beige-and-white uniforms.

With the flyer still in my hand, I move over to the side, out of the way of students who are now pouring into campus, to give it a read.

CHISHOLM IS TALKING

An online school magazine written
by students for students.
Are you interested in writing for the magazine?
Come to the meeting in the library
this Thursday during lunch.

I used to love writing. When I was five years old, Abuelo gave me a journal only for it to sit in my desk drawer for years. The older I got, the more I noticed that Abuelo carried his journal with him and always found a quiet place to sit and write.

Sometime during third grade, I decided to start doing that too. Except I didn't know what to write about in my journal. Writing at school always came with a topic and directions, but writing in my journal meant I could write about anything. I didn't know what to do with that freedom.

When I asked Abuelo, he said he would write whatever came to his mind. So I started doing the same—well, kind of.

22

I mostly wrote about things I saw, like the trail of ants I spotted in the kitchen one time, Pa mowing the lawn, Enrique taking a dirty shirt out of his laundry basket and putting it on, and a whole bunch of other random things. My journal made me feel like I was a real writer. It was a place where I could do me and not worry about Enrique making fun of what I wrote, teachers grading my grammar, or Pa and Ma telling me not to write with slang.

Then Abuelo died, so I stopped. Writing in my journal without being able to see him write in his didn't feel right. That only changed when Evelyn found out students could help write the script for Ravenwood's spring play. She was so excited to act from the script I would write that it made the thought of putting words to paper feel right again. It was going to be my big return to writing, and I was looking forward to it.

This magazine thing . . . I guess I can try to use it as my big return instead, even if I don't know whether it'll work out as well without Evelyn around. It would go along with what Abuela said about joining a writing club to make school fun. I don't really believe the "fun" part, but I know it would make her happy if I'm writing again.

I neatly fold the flyer into squares, slide it into my shoulder bag, and turn to look around my new school. The classrooms and buildings looked so spaced out on the campus map. Now that I'm here, I can see everything from where I am standing. This school is small, and it's kind of a circle.

The courtyard sits in the middle of campus and is nothing special. It's just cement and gray benches, with green bushes here and there. Next to the courtyard is the lunch area. To the right of me are the 100s portable classrooms—for sixth graders. Straight ahead are the real classrooms—the 200s for seventh graders. And behind them is the field. To my left are more real classrooms—the 300s for eighth graders—and the library. And next to that is the administrative office.

Last year when I got to school before the bell rang, I would go to the playground and swing or play tetherball with the squad. I used to hit the ball so hard, the side of my right hand would be bright red and sore all morning. But this is middle school, so even if I wanted to hit a ball around a pole this morning, I can't. There are no tetherball courts; there is no playground; and, worst of all, there is no squad.

While walking to the 100s, I look around at all the groups that have formed around campus. Each has at least three to four people, with one person talking and the others looking at them, hanging on to their every word. I *knew* this would happen; I knew everyone would already have friends. I finally look at their faces, and no one looks like they would be nice enough to let me in their circles—not that I plan on asking.

As I pass by, groups erupt in laughter, and I can't help but feel like they are laughing at me because I'm all alone. And it makes me miss my squad even more. When I get to my classroom, I take out my phone to text them.

Sicily Jordan

This is the worst thing ever

I hate it here already

Alexis Brim

Im sorry ☹

Samara Smith

Me too

Sicily Jordan

Im avoiding everyone. I just want the day to hurry up and end.

Evelyn Martin

I know it sucks. Maybe talking to people will make it better. I dont think there is anything wrong with making new friends.

Just dont replace us 🖤

That's easy for Evelyn to say. She's not the one stranded at Chisholm. But I slide my phone into my bag and look out at all the groups again, trying to keep in mind what Evelyn said. From afar, they don't look as unfriendly as they did minutes ago. Maybe she's right. Having friends here isn't a bad thing, and it doesn't mean I would be replacing the Tether Squad.

When the morning bell rings, I lean back onto the ramp that leads to room 101 and look out toward the courtyard as everyone scatters in different directions. That's when I spot her.

Is that . . . ? No way. Reyna Sado? I squint my eyes and lean forward from the ramp to get a better look at the familiar face as she walks toward the 100s where I'm standing. If that is Reyna, she is just as pretty as I remember. Her perfectly warm, tan skin looks like she just stepped off a beach. Her dark brown hair is now the entire length of her back, and she has a few purple streaks mixed into it, probably clip-ins.

When Reyna sweeps her hair out of her face, I know for sure it's her. She still has her long eyelashes. The only difference is that her eyebrows are now perfectly arched to match her almond-shaped eyes. Looking at them makes me wish Ma would let me get my brows done, but she says I'm too young.

Never in a million years did I think I'd ever see Reyna again, especially here at Chisholm. We were in the same kindergarten class. Then her family moved away before elementary school started, and I never saw her again.

We used to be so close. Our teacher would always say it was like we were attached at the hip. One day we tried to make it happen by sneaking a bottle of glue out from the art supplies. We squirted globs of it into our palms, slapped our hands together, and interlocked our fingers. We ran around the playground and showed everyone what we had done. Once we were back in the classroom, Mrs. Arnold made us pull our hands apart and wash all the glue off.

Should I go over and say hi? Ask her if she remembers me? No.

I can't just walk up to her. How would that look? Thirsty. Like I'm desperate for a friend or something. Hopefully, she'll come talk to me.

Too bad she doesn't. Instead, Reyna runs up to two other girls and forms a circle with them a few feet away from me, talking and laughing.

I turn away and look down. *Great.* The one person who actually makes me want to take Evelyn's advice already has friends.

When I lift my head, a tall, skinny woman walks past me. I catch a whiff of her soft flowery perfume, and it reminds me of those carts in the middle of the mall where a woman sprays you with a scent as you walk past.

"Good morning," the woman shouts, walking up the ramp to unlock the door. "If you are in room 101, come on in."

I'm the first one up the ramp and through the door. The room is completely different from what I expected a portable trailer classroom to be. Each wall has a colored butcher-paper background with a border around it. They are all bare, waiting for our work to get stapled onto them. My favorite is the one decorated like a social media page. Toward the top, it says, *My Favorite Memories*, and there is even a square wooden selfie frame on the floor, leaning against the wall.

"Pick your seats and we'll see how things go from there," the teacher says.

"Cool," a boy with a tie-dye hat shouts. "Travis, come sit over here with me," he says to another boy wearing the same hat.

"Let's go to the back, Trever," the other boy says.

As I take a seat by the window, the boys walk to the last row of desks at the back of the room. I quickly realize that not only are they dressed the same (because we all have to be), but they also have the same face. Twins.

A group of girls come in and take the desks ahead of me and immediately start talking about how happy they are to be together in the same class. And then Reyna comes in, followed by some more kids. When did her family move back here? How does she know people already?

Reyna says hello to the group of girls and sits two desks ahead of me. I watch her every move, hoping she will feel my eyes on her, turn around, and instantly remember me. But Reyna never looks my way.

"Welcome to sixth grade and your brand-new middle school. I am your teacher, Mrs. Taylor." I stare at her as she bounces from her heels to the balls of her feet. "You guys are so lucky. You will be the first to experience all three years here at Chisholm before high school. You will get to be a part of so much growth and change together."

The big window next to my desk gives me a perfect view

of the courtyard. And even though Mrs. Taylor is still talking and everyone is in class, I would rather stare outside at the birds perched on the benches instead of at the slow-moving clock, wishing for time to speed up.

"I have a question," the girl sitting behind me says.

"Sure, what is it?" Mrs. Taylor says, not bothered by the interruption.

"What is that wall for?" the girl says, pointing to the social media wall.

"Yeah, what is that for?" a boy shouts out.

"I'm glad you asked. I will take pictures of you all doing your classwork, presentations, and group activities through-out the year, and I'll hang them on that wall. It will be our class page. And sometimes, I will let you guys take pictures with the selfie frame."

"You're going to let us use our phones in class?" Reyna asks.

"No," Mrs. Taylor says as students start moaning. "School rule: you can only have your phones out during break and lunch. I have a digital camera that we'll use. Then we'll print the pictures back there," she says, pointing to a Mac com-puter and printer in the back of the room.

We all turn our heads to look at it. It's kind of a cool idea. It would be way better if she let us make a real online page. Well, actually, no. I don't want the outside world to see me in this awful uniform.

"Okay. Since it's the first day and many of you look nervous, I want to spend some time getting to know one another," Mrs. Taylor says. "So to start, I'm going to share a few things about myself so you can know me better. Can you guess what country these two things represent?"

Mrs. Taylor holds up a dinner roll first. We all look around at each other.

"Bread," one of the twins, Travis or Trever, says.

"Doesn't everyone in the world eat bread?" either Travis or Trever adds. I'll probably never learn to tell them apart.

"Yes, but this is a specific kind of bread from a specific country. Any guesses?" Mrs. Taylor asks.

The room is silent.

Instead of thinking about the bread, I stare at Mrs. Taylor, trying to see if I notice anything about her features that would tell me what country she is from. Other than the small brown polka dot–looking freckles on her nose and under her eyes, I get nothing. She looks like any other white woman.

"Okay. Let me make this easier." Mrs. Taylor holds up a miniature version of the Eiffel Tower.

"Oh. You're French," Reyna says.

"That's right. My great-grandfather was a marine and was stationed at Marine Corps Air Station Miramar here in San Diego. My family is originally from France."

"Do you eat a lot of french fries?" Silvia asks. I know her

name because it's stitched onto the backpack on the floor next to her desk.

"I don't," Mrs. Taylor says, laughing. "However, I do eat escargot. Does anyone know what that is?"

"No," a few people say.

"It's snails," Mrs. Taylor says.

"Yuck!" slips out of my mouth. The people nearby turn and look at me, as I slide down a little in my chair and then turn back to the window.

"You eat snails?" someone asks.

"It's not what you think. I don't pick snails up off the sidewalk and pop them into my mouth. My family eats sea snails. We boil them and eat them with bread and butter. It's delicious," Mrs. Taylor says.

"That's disgusting," Reyna says.

"People from all over the world eat a variety of foods," Mrs. Taylor says. "We never want to be mean and hurtful by calling something gross or disgusting just because it's not familiar to us. We have to remember to treat everyone with respect. With that being said, I want to know about you. Your first homework assignment is called 'It's My Culture.'"

"Homework?" a few people say out loud at once.

"On the first day?" someone adds.

"She is *trip*-pin'," the girl behind me whispers.

"Calm down. Just listen," Mrs. Taylor says, patting the air.

31

"We all live here in San Diego, and we all somewhat follow American culture. Does anyone know what I mean by that?"

When no one answers, I say, "Like, we eat burgers and hot dogs," in a low voice.

"Exactly. Culture is the food we eat, the clothes we wear, traditions, celebrations, and the music we listen to. And it's all influenced by where we and our families live today and where they have lived in the past," Mrs. Taylor says. "Your assignment is to create a slideshow presentation and share things about your culture. What things do you celebrate in your family? What kinds of foods do you eat? I want you all to be creative with this, so feel free to bring in stuff to show and share with the class. Save your slideshow on a flash drive and be prepared to share on Friday—*this* Friday."

I bite my lip to keep from smiling. I thought Mrs. Taylor was about to make this day even worse by giving us *real* homework. Everyone looks just as relieved as I am. Different conversations start, and the room gets loud as people start to discuss what they are going to do for their presentations. I even see two people high-five each other.

For my presentation, I'm going to talk about Panamá. My family goes there every few years. Ma says it's important for her children to spend time in the country she and Pa are from, so I already know a lot about it. It's my favorite place.

I may not like how my clothes stick to my skin when we're there because it's so humid or the slow Wi-Fi connection in my tía's old house. But the raspado, with the sweet, thick milk drizzled on top . . . *yum*! And the clear blue oceans where you can see red and orange fish swim around your feet.

What I love most is riding the Diablos Rojos—the red devil buses. We ride them when we visit Ma's friends who live far out in Chepo. They are all colorfully painted with bright artwork. When the buses zoom past you on the street, loud music blasts out the windows and all you see is a flash of colors.

I lean back in my chair and finally let my smile shine. I heard middle school was hard work and that the teachers were mean, but so far, so good. I still wish I was at Ravenwood with the Tether Squad, but this school isn't that bad.

FOUR

Mi Familia

"SICILY, THE PIZZA'S here! Come downstairs," Enrique hollers to me.

Before I get to the kitchen, I hear Abuela's mouth running breathlessly in Spanish. Abuela speaks Spanish and English, but she prefers Spanish. She says speaking Spanish is important because it connects us. The *us* she's talking about is her side of the family in Panamá, the one she left behind. Not us in this house who speak English with Ma and Pa, occasionally sprinkling in some Spanish.

"Hi, Abuela," I say, bending down to kiss her cheek.

"Hola, mi amor," she says. Her already small light brown eyes somehow become smaller as she stares up at my hair. "Tu pelo."

I look over at Ma just in time to see her rolling her eyes.

"What's wrong with my braids *today*, Abuela?" I ask,

wishing she had ignored them like she did last time.

Abuela curls her thin lips and shakes her head.

Ma has been braiding my hair for as long as I can remember; actually, since it was long enough for her to "catch and grip" it—as she says. Abuela has never liked my braids. There are only three times in the year when she is satisfied with my hair. That's when Ma flat irons it straight for Easter, Nochebuena, and school picture day. Last year it went up to five times because we went to two quinceañeras.

After I take my usual seat at the table next to Abuela, Pa blesses the food, and then he, Enrique, and I grab slices from the boxes while Ma pours the drinks. Abuela sits watching.

"Abuela, you don't want dinner?" Enrique asks.

"Dinner?" Abuela says. She pushes a pizza box away from her, then slowly rubs the inside of her right palm with her left thumb. The blue veins in her pale hands look puffy. Her arthritis must be acting up.

"You don't like pizza?" Enrique asks.

"What? Why?" I ask. "Pizza is so good!"

"When I was growing up, Panamá didn't have pizza; it wasn't common. I never heard of it or tried it until I moved to the States," Abuela explains.

"Oh, I completely forgot," Pa says. "What else can I get you, Mamá?"

"I'll just have some café," Abuela says. And before she can finish, Pa is up and at the pantry, grabbing the Café Durán.

"Ew, why are there so many veggies on here?" I say, picking bell peppers and onions off my slices.

"Los vegetales son muy importantes . . ." Abuela goes on and on while looking at me. Correction: while looking at my hair. She continues speaking in Spanish, rolling her tongue extra-long and loud when pronouncing words that start with the letter *R*. Pa looks like he isn't listening; I know Ma is. I can tell by the way she lets her pizza drop onto her plate that she doesn't like what Abuela is saying.

"My kids eat healthy, Belén. I don't mind them having pizza every once in a while," Ma says to Abuela.

"So how was the first day of school?" Pa asks, trying to change the subject.

"It was okay," Enrique answers with a mouth full of pizza while looking at his phone.

"¿Qué? You're in high school now. All you have to say is that it was okay?" Pa asks.

"And put your phone away," Ma says. "You two act like those things are part of your bodies."

These days, Enrique is mostly interested in girls, playing video games with friends, and listening to hip-hop. Ma says he acts like a regular teen, so she and Pa don't care that he spends so much time in his room. The only time Ma forces him to come out is at dinnertime. It's important to her that we all eat dinner together every evening.

Instead of responding to Pa's question, Enrique shrugs

36

his shoulders, slides his phone into his back pocket, and grabs two more slices of pizza.

"And you, Sicily?"

"It was all right," I say. "My teacher is cool; she let us pick our seats. And I saw Reyna. I guess her family moved back here during the summer."

Abuela clears her throat. When I look over at her, she winks and says, "I told you it would work out."

"Today wasn't *that* bad," I say. "I mean, I still wish I could go to Ravenwood."

"You were so worried about not knowing anyone, and look, you reunited with your old friend," Ma says.

I shake my head in agreement and bite into my pizza. Too bad that's not what happened. I'm not going to admit that I was too nervous to talk to Reyna. I'm not in the mood for a speech from Ma about having self-confidence and being bold.

"Well, it sounds like Chisholm isn't as awful as you thought it would be," Pa says. "Did you get any homework?"

I go on to tell mi familia about the "It's My Culture" assignment.

"Sicily, don't wait until the last minute to work on your assignment. You'll run out of time and get a bad grade," Ma says.

"She'll do fine," Pa says.

"I hope so," Ma says, twisting her hair into a bun and exposing her diamond stud earrings—a birthday gift from Pa.

"Ma, I won't get a bad grade," I say with just enough attitude to show I'm annoyed by her comment, but not enough to get in trouble. I hate that Ma is always worried about me getting bad grades. I've never gotten anything lower than a B-plus. Maybe Enrique needs her little reminders, but I don't.

"I have a bunch of pictures that you can use for your class project," Ma adds.

"And I can send you some songs to play for your class. You know, some Soca music," Pa says, jumping up from his chair. He starts shuffling his feet and moving his waist, dancing to the Soca music playing in his head.

"No. Not that. Play some reggaetón for your class," Enrique says. "And make sure you tell them reggaetón started in Panamá. I hate when people say it started in Puerto Rico."

"Thanks, I know a lot about Panamá. It'll be easy to put a presentation together," I say, shaking my head.

Pa's biggest cheerleader, Abuela, drowns out my words by clapping and laughing along with Pa, who is still dancing and smiling as his gold tooth shines in his mouth. When Pa was a kid, Abuelo took him to get his gold tooth; it was sort of a rite of passage thing.

"Oh, sit down," Ma says to Pa.

"Come on, you know I love to dance," Pa says.

"Sicily, let us know when you're going to work on your project," Pa says, finally sitting. "We can help you put it together. And your Ma and I can share some stuff with you about Panamá and our family."

"You should take those braids out for your presentation," Abuela says out of nowhere. We all turn and look at her. "Straighten your hair, look professional."

Great. Here she goes again. I never tell her I think she should dye her gray hair.

"Professional?" Enrique says. "Abuela, it's just school."

"Right, it's not that serious. The presentation is a way for us to learn more about each other. Plus, my braids look good," I say.

"I thought you would have relaxed her hair by now, Carmen," Abuela says, glaring at Ma. "Braids are so ugly. They are for girls who have pelo malo that doesn't grow." I shake my head, making sure I'm hearing what I'm *actually* hearing. "I've held my tongue for a long time, ignoring those things in her hair. I don't understand why you allow mi nieta to walk around looking so . . . so low-class and poor and ghetto," Abuela says like I'm not sitting right next to her.

My mouth slowly falls open. "G-Ghetto? I look . . . low-class? Poor?" My voice cracks as I search for more words to say. My palms turn red and get hot like I just touched the face of an iron. Abuela has made comments about my braids before, but nothing like this.

I can't believe it. There is no way *my* abuela just said that about me. Someone or something must have morphed into her body because this woman sitting next to me is not the person whose loud laugh always cracks me up. She is not the woman who used to help me clean up my room so Ma and Pa wouldn't get mad at me. And she is definitely not the abuela who made me feel better about having to go to a different school than my friends.

All I can do is stare at her. Is this really what she thinks of me? Just because I wear my hair in braids?

With my mouth still open, I turn to Pa. His right eyebrow is raised higher than I have ever seen it as he stares at Abuela. I look from him to Ma, with my eyes begging, *Please, one of you say something before I do.* Because now, I have found the words I want to say to Abuela. They are words I know I'm not supposed to use, especially when speaking to an adult.

Pa clears his throat and opens his mouth. Before any sound can escape, Ma stands up and points her finger at Abuela. Ma's mouth starts moving fast while Spanish words fly out like flames. Her lips and cheeks are tight as she speaks. Abuela stands and says something. Ma gets louder and cuts her off.

Yes. Get her, Ma.

"Wow," Enrique says as we watch the two of them go back and forth with Pa sitting in between them.

The last time Ma and Abuela got into it like this was when Abuela tried to give Enrique a tall glass of Seco with lime to calm his cough.

"Hold on, Carmen," Pa says, standing up from his chair. Ma turns to him and lets him have it in Spanish too. Abuela sits down and plants her arms across her chest.

Really? She has the nerve to be upset? This is all her fault. Did she think Ma was going to let her slide after saying those things to me?

When Ma finishes with Pa, she stomps out of the kitchen. Pa goes after her, and I can hear them whispering in the hallway.

I move my eyes away from Abuela to Enrique and stay quiet. My muscles are quivering. I'm about to explode with curse words in English and Spanish (because who doesn't know curse words in Spanish?). I'm fuming. I try controlling myself by sitting as stiffly as possible. I squeeze my eyes shut and try to teleport up to my room or anywhere, far away from Abuela.

It doesn't work.

So I jump up from my seat and run. Run from Abuela's hate-filled words, as hot tears stream down my face, straight into my room. Hurling myself into my desk chair, I stare at the white, blank wall ahead of me. *What just happened?*

My tears are still flowing, and my hands shiver like I'm cold. I calm down enough to grab some tissues from the box on my desk and wipe my face. My eyes are heavy, my nose is full, and my heart . . . my heart feels like Abuela reached into my chest, crumpled it in her hand, and yanked it out of me.

And now, I sit here listless, not sure of what to do or say. Abuela and I just sat together in my room a week ago and talked as she tried to help me feel better about going to Chisholm. Being there for me has always been her job, and she has always done it well. Today that job is over. After what she just said, everything has changed and I'm not sure things can ever go back to how they used to be.

FIVE

Day Two

I'VE HEARD PEOPLE say that after you do something once, it gets easier the more you do it. When it comes to day two at my new school, that's not the case. Today is actually worse than yesterday, mostly because I can't get what Abuela said about me out of my head.

I feel like I'm on a different planet. Like some kind of zombie, I've gone through the day in a fog. A fog filled with thoughts of Abuela. I keep telling myself I'll be okay if I just keep my head clear of everything related to her. That means when I pull out my spiral notebook and run across the school magazine flyer from yesterday, I completely ignore it and push it to the bottom of my shoulder bag.

To distract myself from it all, during class, I watch a girl named Megan mess with the people who sit near her. With her faded, wrinkled uniform, uncombed hair, and the mean

43

boys she hangs out with, Megan is nothing like the other girls in the class.

I didn't notice her yesterday, probably because she was chill. But today, Megan does everything from throwing balled-up pieces of paper and tripping people when they walk past her to tapping her pencil hard on her desk and talking over Mrs. Taylor. She's so extra.

I roll my eyes and look away from her, slip my small circular mirror from my pocket, and check my braids out as best as possible without Mrs. Taylor noticing. They look great. A little fuzzy around the edges because my headscarf slipped off last night, but these braids are not that old.

I am not ghetto. I am not poor. I am not low-class. I do not have pelo malo.

This is the fifth time I've repeated those sentences to myself since leaving home this morning. And I'm sure I'll have to keep saying it until I get over what Abuela said.

"Tomorrow, we will be starting our social studies unit on the American Civil War," Mrs. Taylor announces. "For tonight's homework, research it online and write down five facts. For now, let's head out to the field for a fun end-of-day activity."

The fresh air is a welcome relief from the stuffy portable classroom. The sun is no longer as hot as it was during lunch, and a slight breeze tickles my face. Once we get to the field, Mrs. Taylor explains that she is pairing us up with partners and giving us all blindfolds. Each partner will get a turn to be blindfolded while the other gives directions on how to get through a course outlined on the field with yellow cones— the first team to complete the course without knocking over any cones or falling down wins.

Mrs. Taylor pairs us up randomly and hands out the blindfolds. I pray I don't get paired with Megan.

"You and you," Mrs. Taylor says, pointing at Reyna and me.

"Yes!" Without looking in my direction, Reyna pumps her fist in the air. "Let's do this! I'll go first." She takes the blindfold from Mrs. Taylor, puts it over her eyes, and ties it at the back of her head.

Once the race starts, I can hardly control my laughter. Reyna is running all over the place, not even listening to my directions. She crashes into people, trips and falls a lot, gets back up every time, and then finally crosses the finish line. When Mrs. Taylor sees that more falling is happening than racing, she blows her whistle and shouts, "Give your blindfold to your partner, and we'll start a new round."

Reyna unties her blindfold and hands it to me. Her eyes grow wide when she looks at me, and a big smile spreads across her face. I bite my bottom lip.

"Sicily! OMG, do you remember me?"

"Um, Reyna, right?" I say, acting as shocked as she is. "From kindergarten. Mrs. Arnold's class."

"Yes, wow," Reyna says, leaning in for a hug. "I can't

believe we're in the same class and we didn't even notice."

"I know, right? Crazy." I let out a huge breath and put my arms around her.

"What's been up?" she asks.

"Nothing much," I say, shrugging my shoulders. "When did you move—"

Mrs. Taylor blows her whistle, starting the next round. Reyna quickly ties the blindfold around my head and tells me to "crush it." That's exactly the opposite of what I do.

I end up tripping after almost every step I take. I'm laughing so much that my stomach is tight and stiff. After falling for the fourth time, I give up and lie in the grass. When I finally take off my blindfold and sit up, I see that no one has completed the course this round. Everyone is all over the place, wandering around lost.

"Well, that was an epic fail," Mrs. Taylor says, chuckling. "I guess we'll be working on our communication skills this year." She ends the activity and gives us thirty minutes of free time. Two boys run to the shed on the opposite side of the field to get soccer balls, footballs, and other sports equipment.

Reyna and I sit on the grass next to each other, watching everyone else. It's weird when we don't start talking our heads off like we did when we were younger. Our old teacher never let us be partners and always had to separate us because we were constantly doing goofy things to make each other laugh.

I break our silence and re-ask my question. "So when did you move back?"

"At the beginning of summer," Reyna says, dusting grass off her shoe.

"Oh, okay," I say, trying to think of something else to say. "Hey, remember we used to love green slime?"

"Oh, yeah. And remember when I put a little on that boy Marcos's desk?"

"And then he started crying because he thought it was real snot!" Reyna and I start cracking up.

I haven't touched slime since I was in third grade when I got a clump of it stuck in my braids. Ma had to soak my braids for an hour to get the slime loose enough so she could unbraid my hair and wash it.

When Reyna and I finish laughing, we sit silently. I'm not sure what else to talk about—I don't want to keep bringing up old memories of dumb stuff we used to do, but I have no idea what she's into now. I give her a half smile as she rocks her head up and down and then looks out toward the field. I start picking at my nail polish. I wonder if Reyna will want to be my friend again. Or if she's thinking I'm weird or something.

"So, your braids . . ." Reyna pauses, and so does my heart. I peek over at her from the corner of my eye. An image of last night's dinner takes over my vision, as the words *ghetto* and *low-class* burn in my ears.

". . . I love them," Reyna quickly adds.

"Thanks," I say, pressing my hand to my heart.

"I remember you always had your hair braided. And on picture day, you wore it out, and everyone was so amazed at how long your hair was."

"And they all kept trying to touch it too. So annoying," I say.

"What were those cute hair ball things your mom used to always put in your braids?"

"Oh, some people call them hair bobbles. My mom calls them bolitas."

"Do you ever watch hair influencers on YouTube? I follow a bunch of them. I love it when they post braid tutorials. The styles are so pretty," Reyna says.

"I love those kinds of videos," I say. "My mom did these braids. I'm trying to learn how to do them myself so I can switch them up whenever I want." I slip my phone out of my pocket and look out for Mrs. Taylor. I still shift my body, so my back is toward her. She's far enough away that I doubt she'll see it. "Here are some pics of when I have tried to braid my hair myself," I say, handing Reyna my phone. "They're a little funky. I'm getting better though."

"Sicily, this looks good. Especially this one," Reyna says, pointing to the picture of me with the halo braid I attempted to do last month.

Without thinking, I say, "I can braid your hair like this

too." The words just flew out of my mouth. When Reyna smiles at me with all her teeth showing, I instantly regret telling her that. I mean, I've never braided anyone else's hair before. I can barely braid mine. But if Reyna is anything like I remember, she won't trip if I mess up. We'll just laugh and move on, I hope.

"OMG!" Reyna shouts. "Text me your number. We can hang out sometime."

She gives me her number and I send her mine, thinking, *Yes! We're friends again.* And I didn't even have to take Abuela's advice about joining a writing club to do it.

"And you have to meet my friends Kamaya and Kiara."

"Who?" I ask. My stomach slams down to my feet.

"These two girls who live in my neighborhood. We hung out every day all summer. They go here too. We'll look for them after school."

Reyna plus two more friends is good news. *It should be, but it isn't.* For some reason, I feel a little uneasy about it. If Reyna already has two close friends, I might not fit in with all three of them.

I honestly only wanted *my* friend back. We used to have so much fun getting in trouble together. But I can't fully tell if Reyna feels the same way, and there is no way I'm going to ask her. Instead, I clear my throat and let out a low "cool." I paste a smile onto my face and stare out toward the street beyond the gate that surrounds the campus.

SIX
The Gift

MY ROOM IS still the disaster I left it in yesterday morning when I was looking for my anklet from Abuela. Since then, I have been in no mood to clean it, but I know I have to do something before Ma comes in here again. As I think about how much worse my punishment will be for letting my room go uncleaned for two days in a row, a burst of energy rushes through me like a fast-moving river.

I immediately start stuffing and shoving clothes into open drawers. I lie on my stomach on the floor and push piles of stuff under my bed. While pushing the last of it under, my hand brushes over something cold. I roll my eyes—my anklet. Why didn't I think to look for it under my bed?

I pull the anklet out and lay it flat in my hand. I feel like balling it up and tossing it across my room into the trash can.

Only I can't—it's too beautiful. Plus, I think it's real gold. I'll leave it on my nightstand for now. And if things get any worse with Abuela, I'll hand it back to her myself.

Once my room is fake clean, I sit at my desk and grab a Red Vine from a half-eaten box. Red Vines are my absolute most favorite thing on earth. They are soft and chewy, and I like using them as straws when I drink root beer. Every time Pa sees me eating them, he tells me Abuelo used to love munching on red licorice too. Then he pats me on the head and calls me "little Armando." Thinking about those moments reminds me of my journal.

I open the top drawer of my desk and push pens, markers, Post-it notes, and other junk from side to side. *Ugh*. It's not in here. I open the second drawer and lift a stack of old magazines.

"Ah, here it is."

It's at the very bottom of the deep drawer. I pull out my journal, the one Abuelo gave me. Slowly, I rub my fingers over the dark-and-light-pink ribbon woven on the front and back covers. Holding this journal in my hands for the first time in just a little over a year is weird—a good weird if that makes sense. I haven't seen it in so long. It feels like a missing body part has been reattached.

I miss Abuelo so much.

On the inside of the front cover, he wrote:

I know you have the gift. The gift that allows you to express yourself with words that touch people's souls. Write in this journal as much as possible. Share your innermost thoughts and feelings because writing in a journal is like having a relationship with your mind.

I flip through the pages and think back to the day Abuelo died. I remember feeling like someone had knocked all the air out of me as I came to understand I would never see him again. I felt lost, like I was in a dark green forest searching for him, while deep down inside, I knew that no matter where or how long I looked, I would never find him.

My eyes burned with tears that day as I thought of all the times he picked me up from school and we secretly went to have ice cream without Enrique. How he would scoop me up with one arm when I was little and raise me high into the sky while making airplane noises. How he would burst out laughing at the random jokes in his head, jokes he said were not for my young ears.

That's when I took out my journal and did sort of a brain dump. I got everything I was feeling and thinking about out of my head and onto paper. Once I finished, I felt better—just a little. When I put my journal away that day, I decided I wouldn't take it out until I was ready to write again. Back then I thought that day would never come. And then without even thinking about it, I promised Evelyn I would try out to write the script for the spring play.

My bedroom door flies open, and I almost drop my journal. "Ma, you scared me," I say. *Good thing I "cleaned" in here.*

"I did?" Ma asks. "Why? What are you up to?"

"Nothing much," I say, holding my journal up for her to see.

"Oh, I haven't seen that in so long," she says, coming into my room. "I remember when your abuelo gave this to you. He told Pa and me over and over that you have the gift."

"What did he mean by that exactly?" I ask.

"The gift of writing."

"Really?" I say. "How did he know?"

"I don't know," Ma says. "I guess it takes a writer to recognize another writer."

"I've never thought of writing as a gift. Just something that has always been easy for me and fun."

"Abuelo must have seen your talent. That's why out of all his grandchildren, he gave only you a journal. Do you still use it?" Ma asks.

"No." I look away from her. "I haven't written for fun in a long time. I'd planned on doing some writing once I got to Ravenwood."

Ma makes a face that says, *Don't go there again*, so I don't. "Knowing that Abuelo believed in me so much makes me want to start again—a lot. And you know what? My school is starting an online magazine. Who knows, maybe

I'll be able to write for it."

"That's great. I'm glad you found something to get involved in," Ma says. "Remember: Writing is a nice hobby. But it is not nearly as important as your schoolwork. That *always* has to come first."

I tilt my head to the side and think back to the time I heard Ma talking on the phone about Hudson, our neighbor who plays the piano. Ma said something about Hudson having talent, and that it was a shame he would never be able to make a living by playing the piano.

"I understand. I'll make sure my grades don't drop," I say. "Right now, I'm not sure what I want to be yet. What if one day I decide I want to write for a magazine or be a playwright?"

Ma presses her lips together and sits silently for a moment. "Sicily, your abuelo was so sweet and kind. I miss him. I truly do." Her expression changes from a smile to a look of anger. "He's nothing like his wife, that mean old . . ." Ma's voice gets lower, and I can't hear the rest of what she says. "My point is he spent so much time writing in journals that he never really focused on anything else. He could have accomplished so much more in his life. I don't want that for you. I see you as a lawyer wearing stylish pantsuits to court, or as a doctor in a crisp, clean white coat. You know, a career like that."

Even though this doesn't make any sense because Ma and

Pa have always told Enrique and me that we could be whatever we want to be when we grow up, I don't say anything else. And in that moment, I decide it doesn't matter that it was kind of Abuela's idea. I'm going to try out for the school magazine anyway. Abuelo said I have the gift. So I'm going to use it.

"Anyways." Ma looks down at her hands. "I wanted to see if you need to talk about anything or anyone," Ma says. "I came by yesterday after dinner and saw that your light was off. I figured you wanted to be alone. So, anything?"

I know *exactly* what she is getting at. She wants to talk about Abuela and what happened at dinner yesterday. I spent most of the day trying not to think about that mess. So instead of sharing all the mean thoughts I've been having about Abuela and how my heart has been in pieces because someone I love smashed it, I keep my mouth shut and swallow those thoughts. And it literally feels like something thick and chunky is sliding down my throat.

"I'm good, Ma" is all I say.

"You sure?" she asks. "I know that yesterday must have really—"

"Ma, I'm good," I say in an end-of-conversation tone of voice.

"Okay," she says, getting up from my bed. "Sicily, you are beautiful just the way you are." Ma cups my face in her hands and plants a big fat kiss on my forehead. "If you change your mind and want to talk about it or anything, let me know."

After Ma leaves, I grab a pen from my desk. I don't want to talk about what happened, but maybe I can write about it. Then again, I don't want what Abuela said to me to be written forever in my journal. My abuelo gave it to me for a good reason, so I want to fill it only with good things.

SEVEN

Chisholm Is Talking

I KNEW I couldn't miss the school magazine meeting today, but I wasn't expecting so many other people to attend either. The library's meeting room is packed with people. Some are standing along the walls talking in groups, while others sit at the long wooden conference table in the center of the room, sneaking peeks at their phones. I wish Reyna had agreed to come with me so that I wouldn't look like a loner.

In kindergarten, I used to hate going on the tire swing, but I would do it whenever Reyna asked. She hated when I volunteered to help our teacher make copies or tidy up the classroom during recess, but she would stay in and do it with me. Today when I asked her to come to the magazine meeting during lunch, she said, "Ew, writing sounds like homework," and then ran off somewhere to see Kamaya and Kiara, who I

57

still haven't met. *If Evelyn were here, she for sure would have come with me.*

Ugh. I look over at the door. Maybe I should skip this meeting and go eat lunch with them. It would be great to finally meet Kamaya and Kiara, and to hang out with Reyna so I can get to know her better.

Still, I came to this meeting to see what the online magazine was all about, so I take Ma's advice to be bold and confident. Well, sort of. . . . Instead of interacting with anyone in the room, I stand in the nearest corner and look around. That's when I lock eyes with a boy. He's one of only three boys in the room.

He looks away. I don't. He has dark brown eyes and loose black curls that sit neatly on top of his head. It's his skin that really does it for me. He literally looks like he's been kissed by the sun.

As I'm full-on staring at him, he turns toward me again, and this time he smiles. My hands start to tingle like they are waking up from a nap. I give him a half smile, then look away.

"Hi, I'm Erin Masterson! What's your name?" A girl with purple braces appears out of nowhere, right in front of me. Startled, I put my hand up to my chest. She is wearing a bright orange shirt with the words *We Are Chisholm* written in white and a pin that says, *Rise to the Challenge.*

I look her up and down; she must have a lot of school

spirit. I can't blame her though. I would wear that ugly shirt too if it meant I didn't have to wear our disgusting school uniform.

"Hi, I'm Sicily," I say, unsure if I should have included my last name like she did.

"Nice to make your acquaintance," she says, shaking my hand hard. "I'm so glad you came. I'm the school magazine representative."

Erin Masterson has these light blue eyes that are almost clear—like ice. The way she looks directly into my eyes is kind of creepy, so I keep looking over her left shoulder, trying to break her intense eye contact.

"Nice to make your acquain . . . tance. I mean, nice to meet you too," I say while rubbing the hand she shook the life out of. "I think you're the one who gave me the flyer about this meeting the other day."

"Correct." She twirls the hair at the end of her long blonde ponytail. "I wanted to get the word out about the magazine and get as many people to participate as possible. It's dreadful that the meeting has to happen during lunchtime. However, I'm delighted you came."

"Thanks," I say.

Acquaintance, dreadful, delighted. Who talks like that?

"May I ask what grade you are in?"

"Sixth," I say.

"Oh." She takes a step back and looks at me like I just

said the worst thing ever. "Well, maybe you will get picked to write for the magazine anyway." She pats my shoulder.

I sweep her hand off me and fold my arms across my chest. "What is that supposed to mean?"

A slow smile creeps across Erin Masterson's face, and she doesn't say anything. Instead, she goes on to greet the girl next to me the same way, with a firm handshake and that word "acquaintance" again.

The hairs on my arm stand straight up. "She makes my skin crawl," I say under my breath.

I keep an eye on Erin Masterson until a teacher comes into the room. He drops a stack of papers on the table and runs his hands through his thick, dark black hair. He seems normal enough, but he does make a case for teachers having to wear school uniforms too. He paired a faded Hawaiian floral T-shirt with brown old-man sandals and white socks that are pulled up to his knees.

"Okay, guys, let's get started," he says. "I'm Mr. Marconi. I teach eighth-grade math, and I'm the adviser for *Chisholm Is Talking.*" He sits down, leans back in the chair, and puts his feet up on the table. "I'm just here to make sure you guys keep the content school-appropriate. You students will do all the writing and basically run the magazine. Before I go over the application process and how I will pick writers, Erin's hand has been up since I walked in, so I guess she has something to say. Go ahead, Erin."

"Thank you, Mr. Marconi," Erin Masterson says, walking to the front of the room. Two girls wearing the same orange shirt get up from their chairs and stand right behind her like bodyguards.

"As you all know, this is our first year on our brand-new campus," she says. "Last year, while this campus was under construction, Chisholm took over a few buildings on Ravenwood's campus. While we were there, I would sometimes read Ravenwood's school newspaper, and one day I thought, *This is so prehistoric*." Erin Masterson taps her short French-tip nails on the table as she speaks. "Everybody now has smartphones, laptops, and tablets. So why not do something online? That's when I came up with the idea for an online magazine. And just like they do for a school newspaper, students will write all the content.

"During the summer, I . . . Oh, I mean we"—she points her thumbs back toward the two girls behind her—"consulted Principal Rivas about the idea, and to my dismay, she was against it. So I got my dad involved. He made a call and, well, here we are!" Erin Masterson claps her hands, and the girls behind her do the same.

"This idea was made possible by me." She stops. "And these lovely eighth graders," she adds, pointing again at her bodyguards.

I roll my eyes. This girl can't be serious. This whole online magazine thing sounds like her little pet project. And although Mr. Marconi said he will pick the writers, it sounds like Erin Masterson is the one in charge.

I shake my head and glance in the direction of *that* boy. He's now doodling on his hand. He's wearing a white wristband with a word on it that starts with the letter *P*. I can't see the other letters from where I am standing.

"Oh, also, the administration is selling these a-may-zing T-shirts for fifteen dollars," Erin Masterson says while spinning around and posing in the hideous orange shirt. "If you purchase one, you can wear it every Friday. See me after the meeting for more information."

Mr. Marconi coughs and gets up from his chair, which thankfully stops Erin Masterson's modeling session.

"Ooookay, thanks, Erin. Let's get on with it. Here's how this will work." Mr. Marconi picks up the stack of papers from the table and removes the paper clip. "To apply for a writing position, you need to fill out this application. It asks simple questions like your grade, your reason for wanting to write for the magazine, and other general stuff like that. In addition to filling it out it, you have to turn in a submission piece."

"Principal Rivas wants me to pick students who are going to be committed to the magazine for the entire school year. The effort you put into your submission will tell me everything I need to know about your commitment level." Mr. Marconi's large Adam's apple bounces like a basketball in his throat as he speaks. "Your submission should be 150 to 200 words in length.

"Any questions? None? Great," he says without waiting. "The submissions are due by Friday two weeks from now. The writers picked for the magazine will be announced a few days after. And if you get picked, be ready to write, because the magazine's content will be updated two or three times a week, if not more."

I don't know about this anymore.

Should I get involved in something that might take up so much of my time? Time away from homework? *Ugh*, I sound like Ma. I know I can do this. *I have the gift.*

"Before I end this meeting, let's go around the room. Tell me your name and what you want to write about," Mr. Marconi says. He takes the pen from behind his ear, flips one of the applications over, and gets ready to write.

Without being called on to speak, Erin Masterson says, "I think the magazine should have a fashion or style section, and I want to write for it."

Erin Masterson's friends follow one after another, saying they also want to write about the same topic. I roll my eyes. What do these girls know about fashion or style? They didn't even do anything to make those orange shirts come alive. If I were wearing that shirt, I would have bought it a size or two bigger and tied the front or side into a knot. Or maybe cut it into a crop top and worn a tank top underneath so I wouldn't get in trouble for having my stomach showing at school. Any little addition would have helped it.

"My name is Michael, and since I don't know anything about fashion, I maybe want to write about sports," says the boy I exchanged glances with earlier. While everyone laughs at his comment, I admire his straight teeth.

Three more people speak, and then it's my turn. I rub my palms together and try to think of a topic I want to write about.

I got nothing.

The only things I'm thinking about are the sandwich and Red Vines in my bag. I'm hungry.

"Um, my name is Sicily." All eyes turn to me and my knees weaken. "And, um, I'm not sure what section I want to write for." Some snickering breaks the silence in the room. "I just want to write," I add.

"Ah, spoken like a true writer," Mr. Marconi says. "Well, since you don't know what section you want to write for, your submission can be about anything you want. Just write." He smiles.

I nod and smile back. Everyone starts asking Mr. Marconi if they too can pick any topic to write about for their submission.

"Nope," he says to them. "Stick to what you already told me."

After he finishes taking down everyone's name and topic, Mr. Marconi ends the meeting, and we all line up to get an application from him. I think twice about getting in line, then remind myself that I need to try, regardless of Erin Masterson, me not knowing what topic to write about, and Ma saying writing should be a hobby.

While I wait for my application, I watch Michael. He doesn't join the rest of us in line. He picks up his backpack from the floor and walks out of the meeting room. I stare at his back, watching him get smaller and smaller as he walks toward the library's exit.

EIGHT

So Easy

JUST LIKE MA told me not to, I wait until the day before my "It's My Culture" project is due to start working on it. It's no biggie though. I mean, how hard could it be to talk about me and my family's traditions and stuff?

I drop into Pa's cold leather chair and push the power button on the computer monitor. His big computer screen is perfect for creating slideshows. As always, I stare in awe at Pa's certificates and awards that hang on his office walls. I do this every time I'm here, and I still have no idea where or when he got all of these.

Along another wall, Pa's bookshelf takes up one whole side of the room. It's filled with books by James Patterson, Mitch Albom, Walter Mosley, and many others. A couple of Ma's books are sprinkled in too.

A few months ago, I helped Pa organize all the books by

genre. Once we finished, I decided to reorder them again—this time by color. Now each row looks like a well-organized book rainbow.

In the middle of the red section sit four journals I've never seen before. Two of them are black, one is brown, and the last one is blue. It looks like someone just shoved them in this spot because there was some extra space. I slide the blue journal out and hold it tightly in my hands. The cover has different shades of blue ribbon, just like my pink journal. There is no way this is Pa's; he doesn't journal.

I open the front cover and see:

Armando M. Jordan

OMG, this was Abuelo's.

I flip through the pages. They are all filled with the most beautiful cursive handwriting I have ever seen. I slowly drag my finger over Abuelo's words, wishing I could read them. Too bad they are in Spanish. I slide the journal back where I found it and look through the others. They were also Abuelo's, and they too are written in Spanish. I hold the last one up to my chest, sigh, and shake my head. For the first time ever, I wish I knew Spanish.

Back at Pa's computer, I start my online search. I find several pictures that are perfect for my presentation. After cutting and pasting them into my slideshow, I pick background colors and fonts, then save everything onto my flash drive.

I take a gel pen and some lined paper from Pa's desk and start writing what I will say to my class. Since I'm always texting on my phone, using a pen and paper is a nice change. As I write, I keep stopping to cross out words and edit my work. I want this to be flawless.

Pa walks in and puts a stack of papers on his desk, next to the computer monitor. "Do you need any help?"

"No, I got it," I say. "Hey! How come you never told me you have Abuelo's journals?"

"Oh, I completely forgot," Pa says. He walks over to the bookshelf and starts pulling them out. "Last week, when I was at Abuela's helping her sort through the last of Abuelo's stuff, she asked me to give these to you," he says while stacking the journals on top of each other. "She said Abuelo would have wanted you to have them."

Hmm. Abuela sent them for me. I lower my eyelids and twist my mouth to the side. I don't know how to feel about this. Even though Abuela gave Pa the journals to give to me before she said what she said about my braids, I don't know if I want *anything* from her. But other than the journal he gave me, I don't have anything that belonged to Abuelo. It would be nice to have something that was so important to him, so I reach out and take the journals from Pa.

ℓℓℓℓ

After dinner, I clear the dishes from the table as Ma preps the patacones. This morning, I asked her to make some for my class presentation.

I want to ask Ma why Abuela wasn't here for dinner this evening—not that I care. I want to know if she and Ma got into it again and if Abuela decided never to come back. Instead of asking, I do what I always hear Ma and Pa say: I leave well enough alone and thank God Abuela's not here now.

"Your class is going to love these," Ma says. "They're deliciosos and can be eaten at any time of the day. I'll take an early lunch at work tomorrow so I can come home and fry them so they are fresh for your class. What time do you want me to drop them off at school?"

"Mrs. Taylor said presentations are going to start after lunch, so you can drop them off in the office around 12:30ish," I say, putting plates into the dishwasher.

I'm so glad Ma was able to adjust her schedule at the bank. I don't want to give my class day-old patacones. "Thank you, Ma."

Ma smiles, then shakes her head up and down. "Are you done with your presentation? Do you need any help?"

"No, I'm good," I say. My cell phone vibrates on the counter with a message from Reyna:

Reyna Sado
Im worried. CALL ME!

Since exchanging numbers the other day, Reyna and I have texted after school and into the night about everything we can think of. We practically text as often as the Tether Squad and I usually do. With all our texting, I've learned Reyna and I still have a lot in common. Like, we agree that bright pink nail polish will always be in style, the black Vans with the white squiggle line on the side go with any outfit, and going to see scary movies is a waste of money because you cover your eyes the entire time. The one thing we disagree on? Red Vines. Reyna says they are pointless because they are not chocolate. Anyway, I'm just glad I'm no longer worried about what to say. Our conversations go on and on now. Not like that day at school when we sat on the grass, and I had no idea what to talk about with her.

"Ma, I'm going to my room to talk to Reyna for a little bit. I'll come back and finish up here later."

"It's okay. Go ahead. I'll take care of it," Ma says.

I tap Reyna's name on my phone as I run up the stairs.

"SICILY, I'm freaking out!" Reyna screams into my ear. I move my phone away and put it on speaker. "My slideshow is ready, but I don't have anything to share. And I don't want my presentation to be me talking the whole time. That would be super B-O-R-I-N-G. Are you ready?" she asks, finally taking a breath. "Do you have everything done?"

"Yeah, I'm done," I say. "You gotta chill. Relax." I hear Reyna breath in and out a few times. "Your presentation is not going to be boring. Why don't you bring something for the class to eat? That's what I'm doing."

"Good idea. You're a lifesaver, Sicily! Let me talk to my mom and see what she says. I'll see you tomorrow."

"Hey," I say, catching her before she ends our call. "Remember, you got this, girl."

"You're right. Thanks!"

Hopefully, Reyna will figure it out. I don't want her to bomb her presentation in front of the whole class. Now that I think about it, what if *I* bomb in front the class? I gave Reyna the idea to bring food to share with the class. Is that enough?

I start picking at my nail polish. Do I need to step my presentation up too? I have the patacones for my class to eat, but do I need to take anything else? Something they can look at in person, instead of in pictures? I have an idea; I just have to get Ma to agree first.

I grab the draft I wrote in Pa's office earlier and make a few corrections, then rewrite everything on note cards. When I'm finished, I stand in front of my mirror and hold my note cards near my waist. I practice what I will say tomorrow a few times and even memorize parts of it. I don't want to make any mistakes.

Now, I need my audience.

"Everyone, come to the living room!" I yell, running down the stairs, skipping every other step. I'm moving so fast that my note cards fly out of my hand, and I have to collect them once I get to the bottom.

Ma and Pa come in from the kitchen and sit on the sofa.

"What's going on?" Pa asks.

"I want to share my presentation with you guys."

"Is this going to take long?" Enrique asks, slowly dragging himself into the room. "I'm busy."

"Come sit down. Escucha," Ma tells him.

I plug my flash drive into the side of the TV, and Pa clicks the remote control until my title slide appears on the screen.

"All set." He hands me the remote control. I stand next to the TV and go through my entire presentation for them.

"¡Excelente!" both Ma and Pa say while smiling and clapping.

"Enrique, what did you think?" I ask.

"It was all right," he says. "It's kind of blah though."

"What do you mean?"

"I feel like you could say more. Maybe add some info about important Panamanians. Or things that Panamá is known for," he says, pulling at the few hairs on his chin. "Remember when I said to talk about reggaetón starting in Panamá? Add something like that."

"My teacher didn't say I had to do all that." I put my hands on my hips. "Stop being such a jerk."

Enrique shrugs his shoulders and runs back upstairs.

"Relax, Sicily. If that's what your teacher said to do, then you're fine," Pa says.

"Sí, I think you did a good job," Ma adds.

"You know what would make it even better?" I smile as wide as my cheeks allow. "You letting me wear my pollera." Ma tilts her head and looks at me sideways. Even though I know her answer is going to be no, I beg anyway. "Puh-leeeez, Ma."

"No," she says. "La pollera takes a lot of time to put on. I would have to be there to help you."

"Just try to picture it, Ma." I walk over to her and press my cheek against hers. "Me standing at the front of the classroom, wearing my beautiful pollera, while giving my presentation."

"That would definitely make your presentation stand out, a sure way to get an A," Pa says, slapping palms with me.

"Fine," Ma says. I pull my cheek away and wrap my arms around her and squeeze. "I'll let you take it only to *show* your class. And you have to keep it in the plastic garment bag at all times. I'll drop it off with the patacones tomorrow."

"Ma, you totally missed the vision. Come on, Pa saw it."

"No, Sicily. What if something happens to it? Just be glad I'm letting you take it."

"Okay," I huff. I pick up my note cards, remove my flash drive from the TV, and go back to my room.

At my desk, I open my laptop and search YouTube for videos on putting on a pollera correctly. I know I'll be careful, so what's the big deal?

73

NINE

What Are You?

WHEN WE CAME back inside after the field activity the other day, Reyna asked Heather, the girl sitting next to me, to trade seats. Mrs. Taylor only eyeballed the move and surprisingly said nothing about it. So ever since, Reyna and I have been careful not to talk too much. That way, we won't get separated like we did in kindergarten.

"Hey, so what did you end up bringing to share with the class?" I whisper to Reyna.

"Dessert. These are called choco mangga," she says, taking the top off a Tupperware bowl.

"They look like orange slices dipped in chocolate."

"Kind of. They're dried mango slices. Mangga means 'mango' in Tagalog. My mom bought them from the Filipino market early this morning. Some mangos are dipped in dark chocolate, and others are dipped in white chocolate."

"Yum, I can't wait to try one," I say.

Clap. Clap. "I'm giving you five minutes to prepare for your presentations," Mrs. Taylor says.

People immediately get up and start cutting, gluing, and setting things up. I stay in my seat because I'm ready. A tinfoil-covered pan full of patacones is in front of me, along with my flash drive and note cards.

I'd planned on putting on my pollera after lunch, but I didn't have enough time after getting everything from the office. Instead, my pollera is lying across a table at the back of the room. I settled on doing what Ma said and only showing my pollera to the class. What she doesn't have to know is that I'm for sure taking it out of the plastic garment bag.

At the end of the prep time, Mrs. Taylor stands at the front of the room.

"All right, class, let's get started. I'll choose presenters at random, so I hope everyone is ready," Mrs. Taylor says, looking around at each of us. "And pay me no attention as I take pictures for our class wall. Trever and Travis, you two are first."

The twins get up and walk to the front of the room. When they turn and face us, I notice they've changed into matching T-shirts with three stripes: red, white, and green. I didn't know they were Mexican.

They start their presentation by telling the story of their great-great-great-grandparents' move to New York City from Italy and why their family eventually moved here to California.

Oops, they're Italian.

I laugh at how the twins finish each other's sentences and say the exact same words at the exact same time. But after a few minutes, I lose interest and start making a list of all the things I want to buy the next time Ma and I go to Fashion Valley mall. As soon as the twins finish, arms shoot up into the air. Some are waving around to get Mrs. Taylor's attention. I only look up to see who she picks next.

"Sierra, it's your turn," Mrs. Taylor says, and I go back to writing my shopping list.

Later, I try to look interested while Akoni talks about Nigeria and Ibrahim talks about his Sudanese culture. I sit through Ray, Christina, Eric, Michelle, and three other presentations about Mexico. Mexico is only thirty minutes south of us, so it makes sense that a lot of my classmates are from there. Several people mention that someone in their family came to San Diego because they were stationed at the nearby military base or had some kind of job related to the military.

By now, there is only an hour left until school is over, and about five of us still have not presented yet. Reyna and I will probably get our turn on Monday, which means I will have to ask Ma to make a new batch of patacones. It also means I can eat the ones she made for today. I slowly peel back the foil cover halfway off the tin pan and slide my fingers inside.

"Sicily, it's your turn," Mrs. Taylor says.

Shoot. I pull my fingers out of the pan and wrap the foil around it. As I stand up, a warm wave rises from my feet up to my head. For the first time, it hits me. I have to stand up in front of a bunch of people I hardly know.

"You got this, Sicily. Go ahead," Reyna whispers to me.

I quickly shake off my nerves. I adjust my khaki skirt, grab my stuff, and walk to the front of the room. Everyone silently watches me as I plug my flash drive into the SMART Board and put the tin pan on a nearby table. A small blue circle spins on the screen while my slideshow presentation loads. I go pick up my pollera from the back table and put it near the patacones. With my shoulders pulled back, feet together, and head held high, I stand tall, just like Pa showed me he had to do as a marine in boot camp.

Letting out a small breath, I begin reading from my note cards as my hands start to shake.

"My family is from Panamá. It's in Central America, and it's a Latin American country. Spanish is the official language of Panamá. The country is an isthmus. That means it's a narrow strip of land that connects two larger areas of land, like this." I point to the map of Panamá on my first slide. "Panamá connects North and South America."

As I continue reading, I start to relax, and my hands stop shaking. I don't know why I was nervous. The class is paying more attention to my slide presentation than to me.

I lower my shoulders and bend my knees a little. "Both of my parents were born and raised there. My brother and I were born here in San Diego. And even though we live in the United States, we follow many Panamanian traditions. At home, my parents speak some Spanish to us, and we—"

The rude girl, Megan, who has interrupted everyone's presentation so far, lets out a loud, fake cough. I look over to see her covering her face trying to hide her laughter. I stretch my neck up and stand tall, then finish my sentence.

"And we eat a lot of Panamanian food and go to different Panamanian events at Balboa Park." I click to the next slide. "Panamá is widely known for the Panamá Canal. Here are some pictures of it. The canal is important because it allows ships to cross from the Pacific Ocean to the Atlantic Ocean or vice versa faster. Before the canal, ships had to sail all the way around South America. My mom grew up on the Canal Zone in an area called Paraíso. That means *paradise* in English. The last time I visited Panamá, my grandpa and I sat on the porch and watched a big ship pass through the canal."

Mrs. Taylor bends down to the left of me to take a picture. Before picking up my pollera, I put my hand on my hip and do a side pose for her camera.

"And this," I say, holding up the garment bag, "is a Panamanian pollera."

I unzip the bag carefully, making sure the zipper doesn't

get caught on the fabric. I hold the hanger up high, so the skirt doesn't touch the floor. "A pollera is an off-the-shoulder blouse and full skirt trimmed with lace. The fabric is usually white, and the designs are usually in color," I say, pointing to the orange flowers on my pollera. "Yarn gets woven through the top of the blouse. And these pompoms sit at the top of the front and back." I click to the next slide. "Here is a picture of me wearing this pollera. I have on the full outfit, including the babuchas, or shoes, gold jewelry, and the hairpieces that are called tembleques."

"You look so pretty!" Sierra says.

"Wow, polleras have a lot of detail," Mrs. Taylor adds, snapping another picture.

"They do, and they are very expensive. Polleras can cost thousands of dollars to make," I say.

I lay the pollera down on the table and pick up the tin pan.

"The last thing I want to share is a snack we eat called patacones." I take the foil cover off and pass the pan around. "You guys can try them. They're still warm and there's enough for everyone. Patacones come from green plátanos. Plátanos are kind of like bananas." I click to a new slide with an image of one. "To make patacones, you peel the plátano, cut it into slices, and fry the slices on each side. Next you smash them flat and fry each side again, and then they're ready to eat. I like dipping mine in a mixture of ketchup and mustard with a little salt."

"My family eats these too. We call them tostones," Silvia says, taking a handful.

"These are yummy. They taste like french fries," I hear someone say.

"Great job, Sicily," Mrs. Taylor says. "Does anyone have any questions for her?"

Hands shoot up in the air like arrows, just as someone knocks on the classroom door. Mrs. Taylor puts her camera down on her desk and walks toward the door as she calls on one of the twins, whose arm is waving around kind of in a panic like he will burst wide open if he doesn't get to ask his question.

When Mrs. Taylor opens the door, I can see it's one of the campus supervisors. Mrs. Taylor steps halfway through the door, and they start speaking in low voices.

"Can I have some more patacones?" twin one asks.

"And do you have ketchup?" twin two asks.

I cover my face a little with my hand, kind of hiding my giggle. Before I can tell twin one that he can have as many as he wants and twin two that I didn't bring any, I hear: "Why is your name Sicily if you're not Italian? And if your family is from Panama and they speak Spanish, why are you Black?"

Everyone gets quiet, so quiet that I can hear people talking in the classroom next door. I press my lips together and look around, trying to figure out who asked those questions. Sweat slowly starts gathering on my forehead and upper lip. My stomach is now hard like it's filled with cement. And before I can even open my mouth to tell everyone that my parents named me after their favorite vacation spot, more questions and comments come my way.

"I'm Mexican and my family speaks Spanish. We're not Black," Eric says.

"Black people don't speak Spanish!" Akoni says.

"She doesn't even have a Spanish last name," Michelle adds.

Confusion takes over my mind and I start feeling lost, like I'm trying to find my way around in a pitch-black room. I want to run out of the classroom, except my toes are curled super tight inside my boots.

What is happening? Why are they asking these questions?

"What are you exactly?" Ray asks.

I don't know who to answer first or *how* to answer their questions. I look toward the door at Mrs. Taylor for help. Her back is toward the class, and I can see her hand moving as she continues talking to the campus supervisor.

I swallow hard and pull at the collar of my white shirt. With my thumbnail, I start picking at the freshly painted blue nail polish on my ring finger.

"She's such a liar," Megan says. "There is no way her family is from Panama."

I jerk my head back and ball up my fists. *Who is she calling a liar?*

Finally, after what seems like forever, Mrs. Taylor is back inside and either sees or hears what's going on.

"Ex-*cuse* me," Mrs. Taylor says through her teeth. Her familiar high-pitched voice is low and deep as she says to the class, "Be quiet, now. Let Sicily have a chance to speak."

Breathing is now a little easier. I'm glad Mrs. Taylor finally got them all to stop coming for me. Now what? What am I supposed to say to everyone? I look at Reyna. She smiles and nods. The air conditioner starts humming and rains cold air down on me from the vent above. I clear my throat and wipe my forehead with the back of my hand.

"My family is Black, and we are from Panamá. That's just who we are," I say, with my voice trembling. Mrs. Taylor gives me a thumbs-up and leads everyone in a round of applause.

I yank my flash drive from the SMART Board's side and snatch my pollera up from the table. Trying to hurry back to my desk, I spin around so fast that my pollera skirt swings outward, knocking over a tall plastic pitcher of red juice left-over from a previous presentation. I watch in horror as the white material of my pollera turns red while soaking up the juice like a sponge.

Everyone gasps, and a few people stand up. Mrs. Taylor rushes toward me. Reyna runs to the sink and gets some paper towels. She races over with a bunch in her hands, and she and Mrs. Taylor start patting the paper towels on my pollera, but it's too late.

"It's okay. Just have your parents dry clean it," Mrs. Taylor says. "This juice should come right out."

"Yeah, it'll be fine," I say, hoping that I'm right.

I roll up the dripping skirt and go over to the sink, where I squeeze out as much of the juice as possible.

"MY. MOM. IS. GOING. TO. KILL. ME," I whisper to Reyna once I'm seated back at my desk.

TEN

Enrique Is Right

I WALK UPSTAIRS softly, step by step, to my bedroom with my pollera rolled up in the garment bag and cradled under my arm like a football. Being as quiet as possible, I close my bedroom door and look at the stain that will end my life. The bright red juice has dried to a dull orangish color and has formed a circular shape that takes over most of one side of the skirt. I should have let it soak in the sink at school. That may have helped some.

I pick up my white laundry basket from the corner of my room and flip it over. All my dirty clothes fall to the floor. I neatly fold my pollera and place it at the bottom of the basket, then put my dirty clothes, piece by piece, on top of it and around the basket's sides, so the pollera material doesn't stick out of the basket's side holes. I slide the closet door open, sweep all my shoes out of the way with my foot, and drop the basket down into the corner.

Last year Ma and Pa went on a cruise and left Enrique and me with Abuela. Before leaving, Ma insisted on showing us how to wash and dry our clothes because she didn't want Abuela "breaking her machines"—Ma's words, not mine. Ma hasn't washed our clothes since, and for once, I'm glad.

I take a step back from the closet to inspect the basket from afar. It looks normal, so I slide the door shut and head downstairs. In the kitchen, Enrique is sitting at the table slicing a tomato. I can tell by all the stuff on the counter that he is making one of his "world-famous" turkey sandwiches.

Without saying a word, I pull out a chair and sit across from him. The smell of mustard fills my nose.

"How did it go?"

I want to tell him what happened to my pollera, but I know he will use it against me later. So I leave that part out and tell him how my presentation was ruined.

"The worst part was when I got called a liar. All because they've never heard of Black people being from Panamá," I say.

Enrique piles turkey and lettuce onto his bread. "That Megan girl was probably just trying to be funny. And it sounds like the others don't know the difference between race and culture."

"I should have lied," I say, ignoring Enrique. "I should have said we are from a country in Africa or something. None of the other Black kids in my class got questioned."

Enrique stops what he is doing and looks at me. "Don't ever be embarrassed because people don't understand who you are. People question me all the time because they don't understand how or why a Black person would be named Enrique. I just tell them we're Panamanian. It's not my problem if they don't understand."

"That's true," I say. "I wish I had known what to say when my class was shouting questions at me. I would have been able to shut all of them up if I had real answers to give."

"You know, this is what I meant yesterday when I said talk about important people or things that are specific to Panamá. That might have helped your class understand."

"How?" My voice grows louder. "You wanted me to tell them reggaetón started in Panamá! How would that have helped? Huh? Tell me!" I can't believe he's trying to blame me for what happened.

"Calm down." Enrique gets up from the table with his sandwich. "I still think you should have talked about that. You could have told them about Bayano too. That would have been a good way to explain to them how there are Black people in Panamá."

I fling my arms up in the air. "Who?"

"You've never heard of Bayano?" Enrique frowns at me.

"Geez, I thought you were smart."

"Well, if you're so smart, then you tell me about him."

"Google it." Enrique turns to leave the kitchen, then stops and turns back to me. With a grin on his face, in a whiny voice, he adds, "You're such a know-it-all. You don't ever want anyone's help."

"Shut up!" I yell. "Hey! Who's cleaning all this stuff up from the counter?"

"You, thanks!" he yells back.

I pat the side of my head, where my braids have been itching all day, and stare at the wall. My presentation plays for the thousandth time in my head, and I cringe every time I get to the part when everyone started to bombard me with questions.

Enrique is right. I should have listened to his advice about adding something more. I didn't think I needed to because my presentation was excellent; I did what Mrs. Taylor asked. And like he said, it isn't my problem if the kids in my class understand or not. I did the assignment.

Ugh. Were they just being mean? Or were they *really* confused? Have they never seen or heard of Black people being from Panamá? I mean, there are plenty of us, like the actress who played Ashley Banks on that old TV show *The Fresh Prince of Bel-Air,* Tatyana Ali. And there's also Tessa Thompson, who played Valkyrie in that Marvel movie Enrique forced me to watch during summer break. He told me Tessa's grandmother was from Colón, Panamá.

So that proves we aren't hard to find.

I bite the inside of my cheek. Either way, I should have been able to explain things, explain my background, explain who I am. I have to figure out how I am Black and Panamanian. I don't ever want to be asked about myself and not have an answer to give.

ELEVEN

Why Is She Here?

Reyna Sado

> Hey. Just checking on you after what happened today. U good?

Sicily Jordan

> Yup. Im good.

Reyna Sado

> Wanna come over tomorrow? Kamaya and Kiara are coming. Youll finally get to meet them.

Sicily Jordan

> 😊

I put my phone on silent and slide it into my back pocket. Reyna checking in on me feels good, like our friendship never ended. With a small smile, I bounce from foot to foot toward the smell of dinner.

Once I get to the archway of the kitchen, I stop dead in my tracks. All I can do is stare. I go from shock to disbelief and then to sadness, all in a matter of seconds. My shoulders sink, and I drop my head.

Since talking to Enrique earlier, I promised myself that I wouldn't think about my presentation anymore. I would forget all about it, chill, and enjoy my Friday night by hanging out and watching braid tutorials. But no. All my chill has just flown out the window because sitting at the kitchen table is the person who is about to make my day go from bad to worse real quick.

I greet Abuela with a very dry hello so I don't get in trouble as I drag myself to the table. Abuela shifts in her chair and turns her body toward me. Does she really think I'm about to hug and kiss her? *Not!* I keep my head forward, skip my usual seat next to her, and land in Enrique's chair. I don't want to be anywhere near Abuela, let alone have to talk to her.

Ma comes to the table holding two serving bowls. She looks at me, my empty chair, then back at me. Neither of us says a word. She puts the bowls in the middle of the table. One is filled with white rice, the other with bistec picado—beef slow-cooked until it's tender and has soaked up a mixture of tomato sauce and chili pepper powder. Because of the beef's flavorful juiciness, this Panamanian dish is a family favorite. And I'm in no mood to eat it.

When Enrique comes into the kitchen, he notices where

I am sitting and stares me down. I stare back with a facial expression that begs, *Please, don't make this a big deal.* He kisses Abuela on the cheek and sits next to her, and I breathe out a sigh of relief.

"Here's your castor oil." Pa comes over to the table, stirring something yellowish in a glass cup to drink.

Ew. I rub castor oil into my scalp to help my hair grow faster like Ma used to do when she was growing up in Panamá. I don't ever drink it. When Pa notices my face, he announces that castor oil helps ease the pain in Abuela's hands and fingers.

Ma puts a stack of plates on the table and takes her seat, and we say grace. Pa and Enrique both reach for plates and start shoveling food onto them. They act like they haven't eaten all day.

Once they finish, I stretch my arm out to the middle of the table, reaching for a serving spoon. At the same time, Abuela reaches for the spoon. I pull my hand back before hers touches mine. What I really want to do is snatch the spoon before she gets it.

When I look down at her fingers, I see the top part of her pointer finger is bent a little and curving out toward her thumb. Her arthritis is getting worse. So, to be polite and because I kind of feel bad for her, I decide to ask her for her plate so I can scoop some rice onto it for her.

Then it happens.

She looks up at my braids, and I quickly abandon the idea. My heart starts pounding, and it feels like I'm sitting on tacks, pushpins, *and* needles. I want to jump up from my seat, go up to my room, and crawl under my blanket.

I turn away from Abuela and try to steady my breathing. When I turn back, she is successfully serving herself. I wait until she is done, then put half a scoop of rice and a small piece of bistec on my plate. I just stare at my food.

Why is she here? Instead of shouting my thought out loud, I bite my bottom lip and scrape the chopped onions and bell peppers off the beef to the side of my plate. Then I finally start eating. I'm trying my best to ignore Abuela. It's strange sitting at the same table with her. I don't know how to fake like I'm okay being around her.

"Sicily, how was your presentation? Did everyone like the patacones?" Pa asks.

I stab the bistec on my plate with my fork and bite a piece off it. "Yeah," I say, while chewing.

"Y tu pollera, did they like it?" Ma asks. My eyes slowly open wide, and my mouth gets dry like I've been eating sand.

Chill, Sicily. Act normal.

I pick up my cup of juice and let out a quiet "uh-huh" before taking a sip.

"What did they say about it?" Ma asks.

"They said it was pretty."

"That's it?"

"Can I go to Reyna's house tomorrow?" I ask.

"Sure," Ma says, tilting her head. From the wrinkle in between her brows, I can tell she knows something is up. "Are you feeling all right? You seem very nervous."

"Yeah, you do," Pa adds. "This is your favorite dish, and you've barely touched anything on your plate."

I peek over at Abuela again. She's now using her fork as a broom, pushing her rice back and forth on her plate. She probably doesn't want to eat anything because Ma cooked it.

Worrying about what Abuela *might* say about my braids is one thing. Add in having to dodge Ma's questions about my pollera, and I am shook. I have to get out of here.

"No, not really," I say. "I'm gonna go to my room."

I rush out of the kitchen and up the stairs. Before shutting my bedroom door, I hear Abuela recapping the novela she watched earlier in the day. How can they all sit at the table with her like it's nothing? I know Enrique probably doesn't care, but Pa and Ma? Did they forget what Abuela said to me the last time she was here? Don't they understand that this woman's words have haunted me for the last few days? No, they don't. Because when Ma tried to talk to me about all of it, I lied and said I was okay.

I have to do something. I can't hide from Abuela forever. Maybe I should call her out on what she said, kind of like what kids do to each other at school. How would that work? I can't run up on Abuela and tell her to stop talkin' mess or tell her to watch her back. Ma and Pa (Pa especially) would kill me.

Maybe I'll just keep my braids covered with a headscarf or hat whenever I have to be around her. That should keep her off my back for a while. Or maybe I'll do what she said and stop braiding my hair.

"No. She is not coming over anymore."

I wipe my eyes and look at my phone. Eleven thirty-seven at night. What's going on?

Sitting up in my bed, I pull my blanket up to my chin and stay as still as possible so I can hear everything my parents are saying in the hallway.

"Belén is no longer welcome here," Ma says. "Didn't you see how uncomfortable Sicily was during dinner? I know it had to do with what your mother said about her braids. I don't want mis hijos around her anymore."

"Es mi madre. I am not going to tell her that she can't come over here," I hear Pa say. And just as fast as those words come out of his mouth, they fly straight toward my chest and pierce my heart. *Does he not care about what Abuela said to me? Does he think what she said about my braids is true?*

"She has no one else," Pa adds.

"Send her to your brother in Texas. Let him deal with her," Ma says.

I really want to run to my door, swing it open, and yell, "I agree with Ma." Instead, I grab my phone and text the Tether Squad. I don't want to hear any more of Pa taking Abuela's side.

Sicily Jordan

Anyone up?

Evelyn Martin

ME! Just scrollin on my page.

Sicily Jordan

I was dead asleep. Then got woken up. Anyways, whats up at Ravenwood? Anything new?

As I stare at the three bubbles on my phone, waiting for Evelyn's response, I realize it's quiet now. I get up from my bed and press my ear to the door. Silence. Is the argument over?

Slowly, I open the door a little and peer through the gap. The hallway is empty. I stick my head out. *No.* Argument is not over. I can still hear Ma and Pa's voices from behind the closed door of their room.

TWELVE
Cousins

I FLIP THE visor mirror down in Pa's car and untie my headscarf. Before leaving home, I slicked down my baby hairs along my hairline with some edge control. My headscarf did a good job of keeping my hair in place as the gel dried. But it's time for a style change, so I am for sure washing and rebraiding my hair tonight.

"I'll call you when I'm ready." With one hand, I flip the visor mirror back up, scoop up my clutch, pull the door handle, and rush to get out of the car. Being around Pa is kind of weird today, mostly because I can't get over how he continues to take Abuela's side.

I stand at the end of Reyna's driveway with my head tilted up while he drives away. Her brick house is enormous and stretches high into the sky.

It has a three-car garage, tons of windows, and two pillars that stand tall on each side of her big front door. Just as I am about to ring the bell, the door flies open and someone runs out at full speed, slamming into me.

My body jerks backward, and next thing I know, I'm on the ground.

"Ouch." I pull my phone from my back pocket. "Oh, you are so lucky my screen didn't crack because—"

"I'm so sorry," a boy's voice says. I take his outstretched hand, and he holds mine tightly. He quickly pulls me up from the ground, and I recognize the white wristband he's wearing. I've seen it somewhere before.

I look up at his face then squeeze my eyes shut. Am I trippin' or is it really him? Standing there, wearing red basketball shorts and a white T-shirt, is Michael. The boy from the school magazine meeting. The word I couldn't see on his wristband that day is *Philippines*.

What's going on? What is he doing at Reyna's house? How does she know him?

"Are you okay?" he asks, still holding my hand.

"Oh, ah . . . I'm—yeah. I'm okay," I say, quickly letting go of his soft, smooth hand. Michael flashes a smile and takes a few steps back while staring at me. My heart starts pounding, and I'm now rethinking my simple black shirt, ripped jeans, and high-top Converse. *I should have put on something cute.*

Michael then races past me—his fresh, just-out-the-shower scent trails behind him as I watch him run across the lawn and down the street.

He left the front door wide open, so I poke my head inside. "Reyna? Hello, Reyna?" I get no response.

I walk into the silent house and close the door behind me. My mouth hangs open as I look around. Everything screams expensive. The gold-framed paintings and crisp, clean white walls make me feel like I'm in a museum. I keep my hands glued to my sides. I don't want to get anything dirty or, worse, break something. Not knowing where to go, I call out for Reyna again.

"Hey, I didn't hear the doorbell," she says, coming around the corner wearing a cute olive-green jumper. Her long hair is up in a high ponytail and swings as she walks. "I'm so glad you were able to come over today."

"Me too," I say as we hug each other. "I really needed to get out of my house for a while."

"I know the feeling," she says. "Come on, let's go up to my room."

Crosses and crucifixes of different sizes hang on the wall alongside the stairs, and a picture of the Virgin Mary hangs at the end of one hallway on the second floor. I feel her eyes watching my every move.

I stop in the doorway of a dark bedroom. There isn't

much on the walls. Clothes are all over the floor, and a blanket and sheets hang off the side of the bed.

"Is this your room?" I ask.

"No way! It's my older sister Maria's," Reyna says, pulling the door shut. "She is the messiest person in the world. And she leaves her door open on purpose, just to make my parents mad. Maria's the one who let you in, right?"

"No, this boy ran out of the house and knocked me down. I saw him at school on Thursday, at the online magazine meeting."

"Ugh, my cousin Michael. I can't stand him. Did he say sorry?" Reyna puts her hands on her hips. "Because I'll call him right now and make him apologize."

"Wait! He's your cousin?"

"Yeah, he lives with us now. I hate it." Reyna opens a bedroom door. "I'm surprised he was at the magazine meeting. All he ever talks about are video games and basketball."

"I don't think he signed up," I say, following her into the room. And again, I stop and stand with my mouth wide open. "This is your room?"

"Yeah, come in," she says.

Reyna's room is the complete opposite of Maria's. Her walls are painted different shades of purple, and everything matches perfectly. Her circular bed has a canopy cloth thing over the top of it that drapes down the sides, perfect for a princess. A transparent bubble chair with a glitter pillow hangs from the ceiling near her walk-in closet.

"I have to try this." I slowly back into the bubble and sit while bracing myself in case the light purple chain breaks and sends me crashing to the floor. Thankfully, that doesn't happen, so I move further inside the bubble and start swaying back and forth a little.

"Your room is like something out of a magazine," I say to Reyna.

"Thanks! That's exactly the look I wanted," she says, sitting with her legs crossed on her bed.

I get up from the chair and walk over to the two floor-to-ceiling windows that reveal a long pool in her backyard.

"OMG, you should have a pool party or something."

"My sister and I are going to have one for our birthdays next month. I'm definitely inviting you."

The corners of my mouth rise slightly. I love that Reyna's making future plans for us.

After slowly walking around Reyna's room and peering at different things, I eventually make my way into her closet and admire all her clothes. I thought I had a lot of clothes, but Reyna's got me beat. I grab hanger after hanger, holding shirts, skirts, and dresses up to my body in front of the mirror.

"I'll be right back. Kamaya just texted. She and Kiara are walking up to my front door now," Reyna says, rushing out of her room.

I hang Reyna's sweater back up in her closet and fan myself a little. *Why am I nervous?* Reyna and I are good, so I should be good with these girls too? *Right?*

I hear all three of them laughing while they run up the stairs. Instantly, my thumbs start picking at the nail polish on my ring fingers. *What's so funny? Am I already out of the loop before we've even met?*

"You guys, this is Sicily," Reyna says as they all come into the room.

"Hi," the girls say together, stretching out and singing the letter *I* so it sounds like the letter *E*.

"Hey." I smile and wave. Feeling a little dorky, I immediately put my hand down. My teeth are about to bite a hole clear through my bottom lip as I slowly walk over to Reyna's bed, where the three of them are already seated. I lower myself onto the edge of the bed and force my face to relax as I listen to their conversation.

"So is he home?" Kiara asks.

"Yeah. Where is his fine self at? We wanna say hi," Kamaya adds.

Kamaya and Kiara kind of look like twins, except Kiara wears glasses. They are both obviously mixed, Black and white, with the same wavy black hair tied up in a top knot bun. They talk the same, laugh the same, and finish each other's sentences. They are exactly how Reyna and I used to be.

"No," Reyna says, sounding super annoyed. "Michael is not home, and I'm glad. We got into the biggest fight this morning at breakfast. He's such a jerk, always picking fights with me about everything I say. Even when I'm only joking around." Reyna rolls her eyes and shakes her head. "I can't wait for my aunt and uncle to move back so he can move out of my house."

I want to ask Reyna why she dislikes Michael so much. But the crease between her eyebrows tells me, *Don't ask.* Kamaya and Kiara seem to get the message too. So the four of us move on and spend most of the afternoon eating candy, singing along to Kiara's playlist, stalking people's pages, and watching hair tutorials on YouTube. I'm mostly quiet during a lot of this, still unsure if I'm fitting in with this group. I don't remember it being so scary when the Tether Squad formed. Everything happened on its own, like it did with me and Reyna in kindergarten. Now that I'm older, making friends seems like work. Or maybe . . . Maybe I'm just making it harder than it has to be.

As the afternoon goes on, I remind myself to relax and finally start feeling more comfortable. And without even forcing it, Reyna and I pick up where we left off—being close friends. And since the four of us have so much in common, Kamaya and Kiara match us, like a perfect necklace and earring set.

"All right guys, we gotta go," Kiara says.

"Our families are going out to dinner tonight," Kamaya adds.

I exchange numbers with them, and Reyna immediately starts a group chat for us after we all hug goodbye. I can't help feeling like I'm going behind the Tether Squad's backs by joining a new group chat with three other girls. I know that's not what I'm doing though. It's like Evelyn said, there is nothing wrong with making new friends.

"So what now?" I ask.

"Check this out," Reyna says, showing me her phone. "Briana Raine is one of my favorite YouTubers." Reyna taps her phone screen and a video called "Halo Braiding 101" starts to play.

"Hey guys, welcome to my channel," a girl says. Her hair is straight and long, just like Reyna's. Neither of their hair is like mine—super thick with corkscrew curls when it's not braided. Briana Raine looks nothing like my YouTube fave, Imani Ashley.

This makes sense. Our favorite hair influencers are going to be different because Reyna and I have different hair. While I have to use a bunch of products to get my hair to hold different styles, I'm pretty sure Reyna probably uses the same few products every day.

"Is this how you did your halo braid?" Reyna asks. "The one you showed me the picture of?"

"No, I braided fake hair extensions into my real hair in

a circle around my head," I say. After seeing Briana Raine's video and how quick and easy braiding their kind of hair is, I confidently blurt out, "I can easily braid your hair like that if you want."

"Yes, please!" Reyna jumps up and rolls her desk chair in front of where I am sitting on her bed. "What do you need?"

"I'll need a comb, bobby pins, and rubber bands."

"Be right back," she says.

When I braid my hair, I don't need rubber bands. Ma or I just braid the hair extensions down to the very end and then dip the braids in boiling water, so the hair doesn't unravel. With Reyna's straight strands, I doubt I would ever find hair extensions that would blend perfectly with her own hair. And I'm pretty sure she doesn't want me dipping her real hair into hot water.

Reyna comes back into the room with a paddle brush and a few wide, tan rubber bands.

"What am I supposed to do with these?" I ask, holding the rubber bands up in the air. "And this?" I point to the paddle brush. "I said a comb. How am I going to part your hair?"

We crack up laughing.

"I don't use combs. I use that paddle brush. And what's wrong with those? You said rubber bands. Oh, and I couldn't find bobby pins."

"Come on, sit. Let's see how this goes."

After spending five minutes trying to part Reyna's hair

with my fingernail, I get the idea to straighten out a paper clip and use the end of it to part her hair down the middle.

"So, are you *really* okay after everything that happened yesterday?" Reyna asks while I wrap the wide rubber bands around and around and around the two sections of hair that I parted. "I know we kind of texted about it last night, but are you *good* good?"

"Yeah, I'm good. For real," I lie. Every time I think about my presentation, I feel all the energy drain from my body. I know I will pass flat out on Reyna's floor if I have to talk about what happened and how I feel again. I wish I could erase all the memories from my presentation from my mind.

"That whole thing was crazy. I even got nervous when it was my turn to present."

"Why?" I ask, finishing the first of her two braids.

"After seeing the way they questioned you, I thought they would do it to me too."

"You're Filipino. San Diego is full of Filipino people. They would have to be blind or just dumb to be confused about your background."

"Right. Still, there have been plenty of times when me and my family have been out somewhere and people have said stuff to us. Mean comments that have to do with us being Asian."

Knowing this conversation will bring me down lower than where I was yesterday, I offer an "I know exactly what you mean," and quietly finish braiding her hair.

"Okay, done," I say after finishing the second braid. "Without bobby pins, I have no idea how I'll get the braids to wrap around the top of your head and stay there like a halo."

"Let me go look in my mom's bathroom."

When Reyna comes back, she's holding a mix of long and short bobby pins and even has a comb.

"Really? Now you bring a comb? I don't need it anymore!" I say, laughing and trying to bring a fun vibe back into the room for both our sakes.

"Sorry," she laughs. "I just saw it in my mom's—"

Reyna stops talking. And we both listen to what sounds like elephants stumping up her stairs. Once the noise reaches the top, we hear voices.

"Oh, that's just Michael and probably his friend Kevin. Nobodies."

"So . . . um, why does Michael live here, and how long is he going to be staying with you guys? And how old is he?"

"Ha!" Reyna laughs. "Are you serious right now with all these questions?" I follow her to the vanity mirror and start pinning the two braids in opposite directions so they frame her face. "Please don't tell me you're like Kamaya and Kiara and think he's soooo fine."

"What?" I open another bobby pin with my teeth and continue pinning as Reyna laughs. "No, I was just asking," I say. My face and ears are hot. And my neck is kind of moist like I've been sitting in a sauna.

"This is too cute," she says, posing in front of the mirror. "I need to take some selfies." Reyna hurries over to her phone on the bed. I let out a big breath and smile, glad that I did a good job of braiding Reyna's hair. The last thing I want is for our renewed friendship to end just as it's starting because I jacked up her hair.

I walk over to one of the large windows and stare out at Reyna's backyard. I wonder if Michael is as bad as Reyna makes him out to be. Probably not. Even if he is, he's cute for sure. I'll just have to keep it to myself.

THIRTEEN

I Can't Stand Her

"UGH, IT'S MONDAY," I say, walking into the kitchen.

"You just missed it," Enrique says. He's sitting at the table eating a bowl of Lucky Charms. "Ma and Pa were just about to get into it. They cut their convo when they remembered I was here."

"Get into it about what?" I ask.

"About Abuela. I guess she's coming to dinner again tonight, even though Ma doesn't want her here."

"Remember I told you yesterday that I heard them arguing about that the other night?" I say.

"Well, I guess Pa isn't backing down. For whatever reason, he *really* wants Abuela here for dinners."

I grab a cup from the cabinet and a jug of orange juice from the fridge. "Well, I don't."

Enrique gets up from the table, puts his bowl and spoon in the sink, and leans back against the counter.

"I don't think I want her here either," he says. "Not if she's gonna keep saying things that make Ma and Pa fight."

"Hello, and *we* don't want her here if she's going to be talking mess about my hair."

"Well." By Enrique's tone, I can tell he's about to make a joke. "I hate your braids too. So I don't mind that," he laughs.

I gulp down my orange juice and give him a deep side-eye.

"Seriously," he adds. "I think you're right about Abuela. I wonder what's going on with her. She's become so mean lately."

"All I know is you better watch out," I tell him. "You might be next."

"What are you talking about?"

"Abuela already doesn't get along with Ma. Now I guess she thinks I'm ugly. Pa is her favorite person. She never gets mad at him. So you're the only one left for her to pick on."

"Hmm." Enrique stands there, with his Afro pick fist sticking out of the top of his hair.

"Sicily, I'm leaving. Come on!" Ma yells, stomping down the stairs. Enrique and I immediately cut our conversation short. He grabs his backpack from the table and heads out the door to his bus stop.

Ma is silent as she drives me to school. Without turning my face, I peek at her from the corner of my eye. Her hands are gripping the steering wheel tightly and her eyes are staring straight ahead. I can't tell if she's thinking about something or just really focused on the road. Whichever it is, I'm fine with us having a quick, quiet car ride. I don't want her to bring up Abuela or question me about my presentation again. So I pretend like I'm looking at something really important on my phone and keep staring at it.

When we enter the drop-off loop, I peck her cheek and hop out of the car. Walking into campus is starting to feel somewhat normal. Even though I still don't know the names that belong to all the faces I see, it's getting easier. I pull out my shimmer lip gloss from my back pocket and dab some onto my lips as I walk to the courtyard to meet Reyna. As I pass by the administration office, I stare at my reflection in the windows. Yesterday, I took out the cornrows Ma did for me last week, washed my hair, and rebraided it.

Ma told me I'm supposed to give my hair a rest for a day or two between braiding styles, but after doing Reyna's halo braid, I wanted to practice on my own hair. After almost three hours (because I kept stopping and starting over), I ended up with two lumpy and loose Pocahontas braids. Not bad for a beginner.

And because I've decided not to give in to Abuela and stop braiding my hair, I'm going to leave them in. I know she's coming over tonight, so I'll be ready for whatever she has to say about them.

"I'm not sure if people are using their time wisely." A familiar voice interrupts my thoughts. "I'm thinking we should change the submission due date so students have ample time to work on it."

Ample time? I turn my head in the direction of the voice. Erin Masterson. She's standing with her back toward me, facing Mr. Marconi.

"Great idea, Erin," Mr. Marconi says, as he looks down at his watch. "Send me an email and we'll discuss later." When he lifts his head, he looks right at me.

"Sicily, right?" he shouts. He speed-walks over to me and away from Erin Masterson. His brown old-man sandals make that squeaking sound that tennis shoes often do on basketball courts as he walks.

"Oh. Uh. Hi," I say. I don't like talking to teachers outside of the classroom. It's so weird unless they're the cool teacher. I'm not sure how the other kids feel about Mr. Marconi yet. I know I want to die standing here with him while he's wearing an *I ♥ Math* T-shirt that looks like it has been washed a hundred times.

"Have you thought of a topic for your magazine submission?" he asks. His coffee breath is so strong, it would probably curl my lashes if they were straight.

I back up from him. "I have a few ideas." That's a lie. I

haven't thought about it at all. After what happened with Abuela and my class presentation and being so focused on becoming friends with Reyna again, I haven't thought about my submission at all. I don't want to miss out on a chance to write for the online magazine, so I have to start thinking of ideas. I spare Mr. Marconi all these details and simply add, "I'll settle on a topic soon."

"Hello, *Sick*-ly." Erin Masterson walks over and sticks her hand out for me to shake.

I look down at it and then back up at her. "It's Sicily."

"Oops. Ha ha. Sorry," Erin Masterson says. "It is nice to see you again." She's wearing a pin that says, *Be Friendly. Be Kind.*

"Sure," I say. I turn and walk away from her. Mr. Marconi has already made it halfway to the teacher's lounge.

I spot Reyna sitting at a bench toward the back of the courtyard near the 200s. The area around her is so crowded that I have to squeeze by people just to get to her.

"Hey, girl," I say, sitting down next to her. "Your braids look good."

"I wore a headscarf last night just like you told me to," she says with a finger in the air.

"Good." I reach out and flatten a few flyaway hairs on Reyna's head. "So I was just talking to Mr. Marconi, and—"

"Who?"

"He's the adviser for the school's online magazine. And

Erin Masterson came up and tried to shade me. Acting like she didn't remember my name or something."

"Is that the girl you were telling me about, the one who always wears a pin and uses big words?"

"Yup, that's her. This is the second time she's taken a shot at me."

"What's her problem with you?"

"That's the thing. I haven't done anything for her to be mad at me," I say. "Anyways, let's talk about something important, like me figuring out what to write about for my submission. You got any ideas?"

"Hmm," Reyna says. "Music, movies, memes. Maybe something like that."

"I don't know. Maybe. I have to come up with something soon. It's due next week."

"Hold that thought. I'll be back. Bathroom," Reyna says, standing up. "Watch my bag for me?"

"Yeah, I got it." I latch on to the strap of her bag and pull it closer to me on the bench, as Reyna walks away.

I look down at my hands and stretch my fingers out. My nails look a mess. I should have painted a fresh coat of sapphire-blue polish over them this morning. I'm out here looking dusty, like Ma didn't teach me better.

"Wassup." I jerk back as Michael drops his skateboard on the ground in front of me.

"Geez, you scared me," I say, holding my chest.

"Sorry again about Saturday," he says. He puts one foot on his skateboard and stands to the side of the bench. As he slides his fingers through his curly hair, I bite my bottom lip.

When I smile at Michael, he smiles back, and my heart beats fast like I'm running laps during PE. I turn away from him and fan myself with my hand. Why do I always feel so weird and hot around him?

"Oh gosh," I say under my breath. "Not her again." Erin Masterson walks over with her little crew of bodyguards, stands right in front of Michael, and starts running her mouth. *Blah-blah-blah*. I take out my phone and start scrolling while praying for the bell to ring.

"Come sit with us eighth graders over there, Michael," Erin Masterson says, pointing to the side.

"Nah. I'm going to get a cookie before class starts," Michael says. "You want one, Sicily?"

"No, I'm good," I say, as my cheeks burn. If I had lighter skin, it would for sure be red or a pretty bright shade of pink.

"I'll go with you," Erin Masterson says.

Michael ignores her. He bends down to pick up his skateboard and smiles at me when our eyes are level. I tilt my head and rub the top of my ear before smiling back at him. "See ya," he says, then walks away.

"I can't believe he wanted to buy her a cookie," Erin Masterson says under her breath. I turn my head away and ignore her like Michael just did.

"Michael is way too cute to be hanging around you," Erin Masterson says, loud enough for me and others to hear, then giggles with her followers. "Besides, your braids are ugly."

My head spins toward her.

All I can get to come out of my mouth is "What?"

Erin Masterson's words hit hard and land on a bruise that hasn't started to heal.

"What did you say?" Reyna appears out of nowhere like Superwoman, walks right up into Erin Masterson's face, and stares straight into her eyes.

"And you are?" Erin Masterson asks.

"Don't worry about that. If you have a problem with my friend, then you have a problem with me," Reyna says.

"Oooohhhhhhhhh!" somebody shouts. A small crowd gathers around Erin Masterson and Reyna. A few people take out their cell phones and start recording. I stand up but don't move. I glare at Erin Masterson, waiting to see what she's going to do or say next. If she and Reyna fight, do I jump in? Do I break them up? Not wanting my friend to become a viral video, I pull Reyna back just as the morning bell rings.

"Let's get going, folks," a campus supervisor shouts to the crowd.

"Have a splendid day, Mr. Webster," Erin Masterson says to him. She walks away, twirling her ponytail around her finger.

"OMG, what happened?" Kamaya asks. She and Kiara come rushing over to us.

"Just some shady girl who keeps messing with Sicily," Reyna says.

"You mean Erin. I've heard about her," Kiara says, wiping her glasses. "Last year, she got a bad grade on something and cried in front of the whole class, begging the teacher to change it. When that didn't work, Erin brought her dad to school the next day. I guess he yelled at the teacher or principal or something because I heard the teacher ended up changing her grade. Then Erin was switched to another class."

"I heard about that too," Kamaya says. The two of them pair up and walk together in front of Reyna and me. Kamaya is so tall that she could totally be a model. Walking next to Kiara, the two of them look like a capital and lowercase letter *I*.

"I also heard her dad donates a lot of money to the school district. That's why teachers give Erin whatever she wants," Kamaya says. "She's just a mean spoiled brat who loves sucking up. Such a weirdo."

"I know, right?" Kiara says. "Whenever she can't get her way, she tells Daddy." The two of them turn back to Reyna and me. "See you at break," they say, then head off to their classroom. Reyna and I wave goodbye to them and walk to our class.

"Don't worry about Erin," Reyna says. "You heard what Kamaya said. She's a brat."

"True. I'm going to get her back, though," I say.

"Really, how?"

"They're picking only ten people to write for the magazine. And I'm planning to write the best submission ever. Erin Masterson will explode when they choose me."

"You think that's gonna work?"

"Yup, the magazine is her life. You should have seen her at the meeting. Trust me. It'll get to her." I loop my arm around Reyna's as we continue walking. I try to keep my face from showing that I'm a little worried. I actually have some doubt about the whole online magazine thing because I haven't come up with a topic for my submission.

"Anyways, thanks for having my back with Erin Masterson."

"No problem. I got you," Reyna says. "I got bullied last year—a lot. After a few months of it, I finally told my sister. She told me I had to toughen up and defend myself. And it worked. My bully left me alone." Reyna turns and smiles at me as we join the rest of the students waiting by our classroom for Mrs. Taylor. "I wanted to stop Erin before she even thinks she can start bullying you. Plus, I owe you."

"Good morning, everyone," Mrs. Taylor says as she walks up the ramp to unlock the door. Reyna and some students follow her into the classroom.

"What? Why?" I ask, moving fast to stay close enough to Reyna so I can hear her response.

"I feel bad for not saying anything when everyone was

coming at you during your presentation." Reyna raises her voice as she looks around at our classmates, as more of them enter the room. "I should have stopped them too."

"No worries, girl. It wasn't you're fault." *It was mine.*

I hug myself as I take my seat. The classroom is freezing, so I shiver all throughout the usual morning routine of the Pledge of Allegiance and school announcements. This is done over a live broadcast and projected to us on the SMART Board. Mrs. Taylor then goes on to talk about Shirley Chisholm and why our school is named after her: she was the first Black woman elected to Congress and the first Black person and first woman to run for president.

"I want to see you all taking notes," Mrs. Taylor says. "A great way to remember new things is by writing them down."

Whenever I have to do a book report, Ma makes me pick a Black person who either invented something or was the first to do something. Since I learned and wrote about Shirley Chisholm two years ago, I stare out the window and ignore Mrs. Taylor.

For some reason, what she said about writing things down to remember them reminds me of the conversation I had with Enrique about my presentation. He told me to Google Bayano, which I regret forgetting to do. I rest my elbow on my desk and hold my forehead in my palm. My mind has been focused on all the wrong things lately, like Abuela. Instead, I need to for sure start Googling things about Panamá and my culture every day. I'll do what Mrs. Taylor said and write things down, so I learn (and remember) more about where I come from and who I am. And I know exactly where I can write everything—in my journal from Abuelo.

Thinking about Abuelo makes me think of Abuela again. I wish I could forget what she said to me. Trying to only makes me remember what Erin Masterson said too. Maybe, just maybe, Abuela is right. Maybe I am too old for braids. But all my friends wear their hair in braids. Well, at least all my Black friends at Ravenwood do. Here at this school, I stick out like a dot on paper.

I shake my head and turn toward Reyna. She lifts her hand to show me she is drawing in her notebook instead of listening. If it weren't for her, I would have looked dumb, just sitting there while Erin Masterson talked about me. I'm glad Reyna had my back, and I'm even happier that we're friends.

FOURTEEN

Timelines

BOING! BOING! MY phone has been alerting me of text messages ever since I got home from school. Reyna and I have been texting about everything we can think of before starting our homework.

When she tells me she's going to the store with her mom and will text me later, I tap on my favorite app and lie down on my bed. Evelyn has posted a bunch of pictures. I scroll down her page, commenting on her photos with different emojis when a direct message pops up on my screen, and I roll over on my stomach to read it.

EvTheDiva

Hey, gurl! Whats up! Any cute boyz at your school? Do you have a BF yet? Miss u 😊

Hiiiiiiiiiii Ev!!! I miss u too. There are a few cute boyz. Its whatever. A BF? No way, school just started LOL. Anywayz I saw u and the squad looking super cute in the pics you posted. Luv ur new feed-in braids.

EvTheDiva

Thankz, u know Im over here at Ravenwood killin it with all the outfits we planned out. I can't believe u don't have a BF yet. All of us have one now. Samara is with Herald, Alexis is with Will. Remember him? He was in our class last year. And I'll have a BF by the end of the week. If you were at Ravenwood, u'd prob have a BF by now 2.

StylishSicilyJ

There is this boy named Michael. He's cute. We've talked a few times.

EvTheDiva

I knew it!!!! I knew there was some1. We're in middle school now. Boyfriends are a must. Next time we hang out you have to tell me everything.

I click on some of the tagged names in one of Evelyn's pictures and go to the pages of my other Ravenwood friends.

Do they all *really* have boyfriends like Evelyn said? Alexis, Samara, and even Monique and Amber have all posted pictures of themselves hugged up on a boy. When did all of this happen? I've been so caught up in everything else, I haven't fully read through everything the girls have been putting in our group chat. *Wow,* I guess I've missed a lot.

When I go back to my home page, I see Evelyn has posted something new to her profile's stories. It's a video of a boy I've never seen before sitting on a lunch table trying to rap. The camera then flips to the front screen, and Evelyn's face appears. She has a huge cheesy smile on her face. This must be her soon-to-be boyfriend.

EvTheDiva

HELLLLLLOOOOOOOOOOOOOOOO!
Where'd u go?

StylishSicilyJ

Oh sorry. Hey, let's chat later. I
have a lot of homework to do.

EvTheDiva

ok. I gotta go stalk this boy's page.
bye. Luv ya!

I shake my head and walk over to my desk, where I have everything I need to do my homework: a few oatmeal raisin cookies, a can of root beer (with a Red Vine straw), and my phone blasting the random songs from a playlist Reyna shared with me.

AMERICAN CIVIL WAR TIMELINE OF 1861.
Use your social studies book and online research
to fill in the timeline of events.

The worksheet Mrs. Taylor handed out this afternoon is blank, with only a bold black line down the middle of it. Along that line are the months of the year. I'm supposed to write about what happened during each month in 1861. Instead of thinking about magazine submission ideas, I should have been paying attention when Mrs. Taylor talked about this stuff today. I do remember her saying something about Northern and Southern states going to war because the South didn't want slavery to end.

I'll figure this out. I always do. Unlike for Enrique, school is super easy for me. I usually never have any trouble staying focused or understanding what I'm learning. I have no problem doing my homework and getting good grades. My fourth-grade teacher noticed how quickly I would catch on and recommended I move up to fifth grade, but Ma and Pa said no. "You need to stay with kids your age," Ma said. "It's about the experience," Pa added. Whatever that means.

I flip open my big blue social studies book and start filling in my timeline.

- **January 1861**: Eleven states break apart from the United States of America and form the Confederate States of America. They do this to be separate from President Lincoln, who is known for being against slavery.

Not a month goes by without the news showing shaky cell phone videos of Black people being harassed, shot, or murdered because of the color of our skin. After seeing these videos and hearing these news reports over and over, I asked Pa why it keeps happening. He said the actions of the white people and non-Black people of color who do this to us can be traced back to when Black people were thought of as less than, not equal, not even seen as human—a time when Black people were used as free labor and mistreated.

I could probably spend the rest of my life creating a timeline of all the bad things Black people have experienced just because of our skin color. I would have to start way before the American Civil War though. And that timeline would span right up to a few weeks ago when a white woman down the street yelled at three Black boys for skateboarding on the sidewalk in front of her house. It's crazy that all of this has to do with the fact that my skin—Black skin—is different.

And what about Panamá? Were Black people there also treated like this back in the day? I mean, can I create the same timeline for Panamá too? And what about Abuela? Where would I put her on that timeline? When did looking different or having a different hairstyle become wrong or bad to her?

I tap my pen on the desk and bite my bottom lip. What's going to happen to my relationship with Abuela? She's probably never going to accept my braids, which means she will never fully accept me. I swallow hard and try to ignore the heaviness I feel in my heart. Will she and I have to go to war against each other? If so, I have no problem doing that, because I have to stand up for what I know is right.

- **June 1861:** Half of Virginia disagrees with the Confederacy. They split from the rest of Virginia, become West Virginia, and join the United States of America.

"What is going on?" Pa shouts from my doorway. "You and Enrique having a competition to see who can play their music the loudest?"

Enrique and I blast music in the house all the time after school when Pa and Ma are still at work. We turn everything off before they get home at about 4:30 p.m. Pa must have left work early today.

"Sorry, Pa. I'll turn it down," I say, picking up my phone.

"I don't know how you kids do homework with all this tontería playing so loud."

"Pa, it's not nonsense."

"I hope you know your schoolwork like you know those songs," he says, closing my bedroom door.

Before I can put my phone back down, it lights up with notifications that Evelyn is still posting on her page—probably more pictures and videos of that boy. This is so weird because last year, we hated the boys. All they did was put their fingers up their noses and chase us around, trying to touch us with their booger fingers. *Yuck!* We couldn't stand any of them. Now all those same boys are cute? I don't know about that. Then again, Evelyn seems so sure. Is that how I should be acting with Michael? Should my socials be full of pictures of him?

I feel like I got left out of a secret meeting that the Tether Squad forgot to invite me to, where they learned about the importance of having a boyfriend. Or maybe I just need to read what they've been saying in our group chat lately for clues. Why else would all this be so easy for them, while I feel like crushes and liking boys has come out of nowhere? I wish I could be as up-front as Evelyn and the rest of them; they are so bold.

Another text notification pops up on my screen. This time it's from Enrique.

Enrique Jordan

time for dinner

Ma hates that Enrique and I text each other when we are

126

in the same place. "Just get up and talk to each other," she says. But we still do it anyway. Staring down at my phone screen, I can see that Enrique is typing something.

When he finally presses Send, all he says is:

Enrique Jordan

u kno who is here

I grab my edge control and a small brush and quickly start laying down my baby hairs that have curled up throughout the day. I shove my finger into the edge control jar and slide the thick, light-green glob down my middle part, laying down the stray hairs that may be sticking out of my two braids. The last thing I want is to give Abuela any reason to shoot comments at me about my hair.

Don't be afraid of going to war, Sicily.

Oh no. I'm not running away from Abuela anymore. Facing myself in the mirror, I flare my nostrils a few times. I squeeze my eyebrows together and practice a squint of disapproval. I open my mouth and press my teeth tightly together in case I get told to smile.

"Hi, Abuela," I practice saying through my teeth. "Hi, Abuela," I say again, toneless, without moving my face.

Okay. I think I'm ready for her—kind of. I slide my palms down my pant legs to dry the moisture I feel. Then I crack my knuckles, grab my phone, and head out for battle.

FIFTEEN

Battle

THUMP. THUMP. THUMP.

I stomp down each step so I can drown out Abuela's loud voice, which is stabbing my eardrums. I cringe and shiver as she laughs and speaks in Spanish.

In the kitchen, everyone is seated at the table. Enrique looked out for me and took my old spot next to Abuela. I smile and pull out the chair next to him. I realize I'm pulling it too hard because the chair's legs drag on the tile floor and make a screeching sound that causes everyone to look up at me.

"Sorry." I sit down with my back straight and my chin up high. I rub my hands together under the table and look at Abuela.

It's time for war.

"What are we having?" I ask, staring at Abuela. She looks

at me, and I become stiff, stone-faced. I'm ready for her. But she just smiles.

Don't fall for her tricks, Sicily. Remember, she's the enemy.

I roll my eyes so hard that I can feel my eyeballs strain.

"We're having sancocho," Ma says.

"It looks like soup to me," Enrique says, peering into the bowl in the middle of the dinner table.

"It is. Abuela used to make this all the time when I was your age," Pa says. He pats Abuela's shoulder, and they smile at each other.

"Oh gosh," I whisper under my breath and roll my eyes again.

After Pa finishes saying grace, Ma puts the long spoon into the bowl, stirs the soup around a few times, and then fills bowls for Enrique and me.

"Be careful," she says, handing me mine.

I shove my spoon into my bowl and start pushing corn on the cob, vegetables, and potatoes around, searching for pieces of chicken. After finding a piece, I shove my spoon into my mouth and chew hard and loud. From the corner of my eye, I see Enrique looking at me. He hates it when people chew loudly. Oh well, I have to stay ready. Abuela can strike at any moment, from any angle. I don't know what she might say to me, so Enrique will just have to deal with it.

When Abuela reaches for the spoon and tries to fill her

bowl with sancocho, I notice she is wearing gloves made out of stretchy spandex material—very different from the warm fuzzy gloves I wear when it's cold outside. I guess Abuela's gloves are supposed to help ease her arthritis, but it doesn't look like they are working. She is trying to hold a bowl with one hand and attempting to grip the serving spoon with the other. Neither hand is bending fully around what she's trying to hold, and the gloves look like they're making things worse instead of better.

She's struggling as if she were learning how to dish her food for the first time.

Focus, Sicily. No sympathy for her.

Pa takes the bowl from Abuela, fills it, and places it in front of her.

"How was school today?" Pa asks.

"Nothing special," Enrique says.

"Are you ever going to have anything to tell us about school?" Ma asks.

"No, it's just school, Ma," he says.

I continue eating and watching Abuela. She's eating with a smile on her face, probably laughing at my hair in her mind. When she looks over at me, I squeeze my eyebrows together and lower my eyelids, just like I practiced in the mirror. Abuela opens her mouth like she's about to say something, so I open mine too, ready to cut her off. Again, she just smiles and continues eating.

What is she up to?

"And you?" Pa asks me. "What's new? You always have something to share with us."

I open my mouth to speak, pause, and then shut it. Anything I say right now may make Abuela attack.

Stay ready, Sicily.

I tell Pa about the online school magazine and some of the ideas I came up with for my submission.

"¿Qué magazine?" Abuela asks. I look away from her and say nothing.

"Good, Sicily. I'm glad you're going to do it," Ma says, ignoring Abuela too. *Yes, I love it when Ma is on my team.* Now we both can overthrow *our* enemy. "Just remember school comes first."

"I agree with Ma, Sicily," Pa says. "While the magazine is a good after-school activity, your education is important so you can get into college and get a good job."

Now it feels like I'm the one under attack.

"No worries, I can handle it," I say and then raise my voice so everyone can hear what I'm about to say next. "Plus, my favorite person, *Abuelo*, said I have a gift for writing." When I mention Abuelo, Abuela's shoulders drop, and she puts her head down. I'm sure she misses him a lot. It must be hard for her to live alone in the house they shared.

After rubbing her eyes, Abuela asks again, "¿Qué magazine?"

Focus, Sicily. Stay strong.

"So, Ma, how was work today?"

"Um," Ma looks at me, probably shocked that I'm asking about her job. "It was fine. Thanks for asking."

Abuela lowers her head again, examining her hands. She starts sniffling like she is about to cry. I'm not sure who is doing too much right now: me or the pain in her hands.

Do I retreat or go harder?

"Did you take your pills today?" Pa asks when he notices what Abuela is doing.

"Belén, do you need an ice pack or something?" Ma asks.

I snap my head around to look at Ma.

No, don't fall for it. She's trying to trick us.

Spanish words drift softly out of Ma's mouth. So much for Ma not wanting Abuela to come over here anymore.

I need to stop this Abuela lovefest now. I drop my spoon into my bowl. Even though the clink of the metal hitting glass is loud, it doesn't take the focus off Abuela. I start tapping my fingers on the table. And not in the cute way, where one finger taps after the other. I tap all four fingers, hard at the same time. I open my mouth as wide as possible and let out the fakest and loudest yawn over their conversation.

Pa looks at me and frowns. "Sicily," he says in his normal voice. "Enough!" he shouts. His eyes stay glued on me.

I lean back in my chair.

Yup, definitely time to retreat.

The "game over" music from one of Enrique's video games plays in my head.

"When everyone finishes eating, clean up the kitchen and then go upstairs. We need to talk," Ma says to me. She doesn't sound or look mad. But I know Ma's battle moves well. She's setting me up for a punishment.

SIXTEEN

DM

I LIE ON my bed in the darkness of my room after clearing the table of dishes and putting the leftovers away. I leave my lights off so Ma thinks I'm sleeping and hopefully won't come in like she said she would.

Fingers crossed.

I pull my blanket over my head and get comfortable. In the quietness of my room, I hear a crinkling sound from under my pillow as I rest my head on it. Sliding my hand underneath it, I pull out my "Why I Hate My New School" list. Last Monday, I was all about this list. I'd forgotten about it until now, a week later. I turn on my phone's flashlight, and with a pen from my nightstand, I add:

#6 Erin Masterson

After folding the list and putting it back, I check my phone notifications.

Michael Sado (YaBoyM.Sado) started following you.
Michael Sado (YaBoyM.Sado) sent you a direct message.

I go to Michael's page, follow him back, and click on the message he sent:

YaBoyM.Sado
Wassup?!

Instead of responding, I look at his pictures. There aren't many. Typical boy. There's maybe 40. There are a bunch of pictures of different Jordan tennis shoes. I recognize a few pairs because Enrique has them. Michael has his baby picture posted too—so cute. I wish I could reach into the photo and squeeze the chubby cheeks he used to have.

I click the DM he sent again, and I'm not sure if I should write back. Is he just saying hi? As in, no need to respond, just follow back? Or should I say hi back? He did put a question mark, so that must mean he wants an answer, right?

StylishSicilyJ
Wassup with you?

Oh no. DELETE.

Hey, howz it going?

No, I don't like that. DELETE.

I'm good, and you?

No, that sounds like something Erin Masterson would say. DELETE.

Hi 😊

Shoot, why did I add that smiley face? That's too girly. I shouldn't have sent that.

YaBoyM.Sado

Sorry again for running into you the other day. I was late for a b-ball game at the park.

Wow, he wrote back so fast. I wonder if he had the conversation open and saw the speech bubbles pop up and then go away each time I wrote something and then deleted it.

It's OK.

So how did you find me on here?

YaBoyM.Sado

I heard when you said your name at the magazine meeting last week.

And then I found you on Reyna's page.

StylishSicilyJ

Oh OK. So are you going to turn in a magazine submission?

YaBoyM.Sado

At first I thought it was a cool idea. Then at the meeting all the girls were talking fashion and then it seemed like the magazine was a girl thing.

Erin is trying to change my mind about doing it. What about you? Are you going to submit something?

StylishSicilyJ

Yeah, well I'm trying to. I'm still trying to think of a topic to write about.

I kinda wanna show my parents that I'm a good writer by getting picked. And my grandpa said I have the gift to be a writer. I want to do it for him too.

YaBoyM.Sado

That's cool about your grandpa. I bet he reads everything you write. What's up with your parents though? Do they all think you're a bad writer?

I don't have it in me to tell him Abuelo *used* to read everything I wrote. Past tense.

StylishSicilyJ

LOL, no. They think it should just be a hobby. They want me to be a doctor or a lawyer or something like that.

YaBoyM.Sado

Are your parents from another country?

StylishSicilyJ

Yeah, why?

YaBoyM.Sado

Because mine tell me the same thing. My aunt and uncle tell Reyna and her sister that too. I think all parents from different countries feel that their American kids have to be doctors or lawyers. Where are your parents from?

StylishSicilyJ

Panama.

YaBoyM.Sado

Oh! I learned about the Panama Canal last year.

StylishSicilyJ

Wow, really? When I tell people, they usually don't know where Panama is. And then there is always one person who thinks I'm Mexican because my parents speak Spanish.

YaBoyM.Sado

LOL, I know what you mean. It's crazy.

StylishSicilyJ

Yeah, it is. LOL! So how come you live with Reyna's family?

YaBoyM.Sado

My parents and little sister moved to the Philippines for a year for my dad's job. I wanted to stay.

StylishSicilyJ

I'm glad you did.

Wait! Did I just write that?

YaBoyM.Sado

Me too. Our school has some pretty cool people.

I look down at Michael's last message again and scroll back up through our conversation. The other day Reyna asked if I liked her cousin. At the time, no, I didn't. Now? I think so. I mean, he's cute. And nice to talk to. Does that mean I *do* like him?

Reyna would probably be mad if I did. She pretty much hates her cousin. Ma and Pa would be so mad too. Last year when they found out Enrique had a girlfriend, they made him break up with her and grounded him. Then they lectured both of us about how they didn't move to this country for their children to become teenaged parents. So dramatic!

All my teeth start to show as I smile and continue rereading our conversation. This is kind of a weird feeling. A feeling I've never had before. Do I *really* have a crush on him?

SEVENTEEN

Black Panamanian

MICHAEL AND I exchange phone numbers and then move our conversation from DMs to texts. We cover everything from our favorite colors (his are purple and gold for the Lakers), our favorite TV shows, movies, songs, and my love for Red Vines. Just as I finish telling him about the disaster that was once my beautiful pollera, the light suddenly switches on and my eyes sting, trying to adjust to the brightness.

"Get up!" Ma says.

I push the blanket off my head and see Ma and Pa standing in the doorway. Great, here we go. I've been in the dark, under my blanket for the last two hours, texting with Michael and scrolling through all my friends' pages. Mostly, I've been hiding from Ma. I guess I was so into what I was doing that I didn't hear them coming down the hall.

"Sit up. Now!" Ma says. She's wearing her floral bata and

has a head full of pink plastic hair rollers. I bet she was all ready for bed and Pa reminded her about the talk she said we needed to have.

"Can it wait until tomorrow? I'm kinda tired," I say, rubbing my eyes for effect.

"No," Pa says. His voice is sharp as he stands near the door with his arms crossed tightly. There are two deep creases between his eyebrows as he stares at me.

I sit up in bed, ready to take my punishment. Whatever it is, it will be worth it. I had to stand up for myself and I did. Well, actually, I was kind of rude. But that's not the point. Abuela has to know that she can't call me names.

"Sicily, it's past nine," Ma says. "Why aren't you wearing your pajamas? Or your headscarf? What have you been doing?"

I push the sleep button on the side of my phone and slide it under my blanket before shrugging my shoulders.

"The way you treated Abuela tonight was unacceptable," Pa says, getting straight to the point. "You know she's going through a lot. She's still grieving for your abuelo, and her arthritis is getting worse by the day." Pa starts walking back and forth from one end of my room to the other with his hands in his pockets. His usually light-skinned face is slightly red, and the dimple that sits on his cheek, regardless of whether he's smiling, is nowhere to be found.

"Hold on," Ma says. She puts her palm up toward him. Pa

takes a deep breath and goes back to his original spot near the door. This is weird. Ma is usually the one who goes hard on Enrique and me. And Pa is usually the softy. We know that with him, we can talk our way out of any trouble we've gotten ourselves into.

"What's going on with you lately?" Ma asks. "You skipped your favorite meal, and you've been unusually quiet around the house. Did something happen with one of your friends? Or did you get a bad grade on an assignment?"

"Everything is fine," I lie.

"Sicily," Ma holds my chin in her hand and moves my face toward hers. "We know everything is *not* fine. I know your Abuela can be a lot sometimes. You still have to respect her, no matter what."

The small, tiny hairs on the back of my neck stand at attention. Ma can't be serious right now. *Respect.* Was Abuela respectful when she called me low-class, poor, and ghetto? Or when she said braids are for people who have bad hair?

"The way you treated Abuela tonight will never happen again," Ma continues. "The way you rolled your eyes and ignored her when she was talking to you. Oh, and don't think for a second that I didn't catch you staring her down."

My heart starts beating so loudly I can hear it in my ears, which makes it feel like steam is shooting out of them like in a cartoon. My stomach is rumbling, and I feel like my dinner is trying to climb up my throat.

"That's right," Pa chimes in. "I don't want to see that ever again. Understood?"

And then it happens—an eruption. Instead of food, words flow out of my mouth, as if they were connected side by side on a string. "Yes, I understand that I have to respect Abuela, but you guys always say to get respect, you have to give it."

Breathe in.

"She wasn't respectful when she called me names last week. She pretty much called me ugly. And I didn't say anything back to her because I knew I wasn't supposed to."

Breathe in.

"So I stayed quiet, and it's not fair. It's not fair that Abuela gets to say those things to me, and I can't say anything back to her."

"You know what?" Ma says, then pauses. "You're right." She tilts her head to the side and looks at Pa. She adds, "It's *not* fair at all."

Pa takes a deep breath. As his chest rises with air, he closes his eyes. "The last few months have been hard for Abuela," Pa says.

"You always take her side," I say. "You didn't even call her out when she said all that stuff to me." I look down at my hands and start picking at my nail polish. Ma quickly puts her hand on top of mine to stop me. She hates when I pick at my polish. She says walking around with chipped nail polish should be a crime.

"You didn't even have my back when Ma told you Abuela shouldn't come over here anymore. It's like you don't care about what she said about me."

Pa rubs his hand over his mouth and looks up to the ceiling. After taking another deep breath, he says, "I've been so focused on making sure everything is easy and perfect for Abuela that I overlooked a very important job. My job to protect you." Pa comes over and bends down in front of me. I crack a small smile when our faces are level.

"I'm sorry."

As hard as I try to stop my facial muscles from moving, I lose total control of them. And before I know it, I'm full-on smiling as Pa wraps his arms around me and lifts me from my bed, into his arms. My legs dangle as he sprinkles little kisses all over both of my cheeks.

Before putting me down, he looks at me and says, "I'll never let anything like that happen again."

It feels good to have both Ma and Pa listen to me and understand my side. At the same time, I also feel torn. My heart kind of has this warm feeling, like Pa's words filled spaces within it that were, unbeknownst to me, empty. There's another part of me—I'm not sure where—that feels like there is more I need to say. More I need to get off my chest. Yeah, that's where it is. I feel it in my chest.

Enrique pops his head into my room. "Is everything okay?"

"Yes," Ma says. "Come sit. You may as well join us."

Enrique sits on the floor next to my desk and mouths, "You okay?" to me.

Enrique's question sparks all the jitters and emotions I felt a few minutes ago when I was talking about Abuela.

Breathe in.

"It's not fair that the kids in my class can call me a liar because they don't think I'm Panamanian. It's not fair that they asked me all those questions because I'm Black."

Breathe in.

"And it's not fair that my po—" I stop myself right before I go too far and tell on myself. I glance over my shoulder at my closet doors, double-checking that they are still closed. My pollera is still in there, and right now is definitely not the time to bring up what happened to it.

"It's just not fair," I whisper. I close my eyes and inhale so deeply that my shoulders almost touch my ears. When I push the air out, all the thoughts and sadness I've been feeling about Abuela and my class presentation go out with it.

"Wait, wait. What are you talking about?" Pa asks. He sits in the chair at my desk and scoots himself over to the bed, near Ma and me. "What happened?"

I nod and wipe the single tear that rolled down my cheek away from my mouth. I tell them everything that happened during my presentation, every detail just as it has replayed in my head for the last few days.

"I thought you were cool after we talked on Friday," Enrique says.

"I thought I was too," I say.

"You explained that Pa and I were born in Panamá, right?" Ma asks.

"I did, and it didn't help. And to be honest, I don't fully understand either. How are we Black and Panamanian?"

"First of all. We are not Black *and* Panamanian. We are Black Panamanians," Pa corrects me.

"Oh, I never knew I was saying it wrong."

"Escucha," Ma says. "My family is originally from Jamaica, and remember I told you my great-grandfather moved to Panamá because he worked on the canal?"

"Oh, I forgot about that. He *actually* helped build it?" I ask.

"Sí," Ma says.

"And my family, Abuelo's side, were from Barbados and moved to Panamá, also to build the canal," Pa adds. "Your abuela's family is native to Panamá. They come from what we call the interior of Panamá, inland."

"So both sides of our family are from the Caribbean?" Enrique asks.

"Sí," Ma says again.

"Sicily, the Caribbean is what those islands south of Florida are called," Enrique says to me.

"I know that, dummy."

We laugh. I'm glad he's here to lighten the mood.

"The point is," Pa continues, "our family is Black—from Jamaica and Barbados. They moved to Panamá to work on the canal. And that's how we are Black Panamanians."

"Can one of you please tell her who Bayano is?" Enrique asks.

"Bayano. He was a slave from West Africa," Ma says.

"That's it?" I say, talking to Ma while looking at Enrique. "You made him sound like he was some important person."

"He was and still is," Pa says, sitting straight up. "Bayano was a king in his West African village before being captured. When the slave ship carrying him got close to Panamá, it sank. Bayano and all the others on board escaped and made it to Panamá as free men. Bayano became the leader of the escaped slaves. He trained them to fight, along with native Panamanians, against the Spaniards, who would eventually try to recapture them. Bayano ended up leading the largest slave rebellion in Panamá."

"Wow!" I say. And then I remember I was supposed to start researching information just like this so I could write it in my journal. *I need to start doing that.* I'm already struggling with my magazine submission but writing a fact shouldn't be that hard. Especially now, because I know Bayano would be a great journal entry.

"Bayano and the escaped slaves—who the Spaniards called *Cimarrones*—were so strong the Spaniards couldn't beat them. Bayano and the Cimarrones fought against the Spanish for years until a peace treaty was signed," Pa says. "To this day, there are still many places in Panamá named after Bayano. There's the Bayano river, dam, valley, and lake."

"Uh-huh," Ma says. "There are a bunch of buildings named after him too. There's even a tourist attraction called Bayano Adventure."

"I remember learning about him every school year." With a smile on his face, Pa continues, "Bayano is a source of pride for us Panameños. He's known as the Father of Resistance because he never backed down. He represents strength." Pa smiles and nods.

"He sure does. And not just him. The Cimarrones are also still praised and recognized for their hard work too."

"What does *Cimarrones* mean?" Enrique asks.

"It means 'wild ones,'" Ma answers. "Those who enslaved the Cimarrones tried to dehumanize them with their words and actions, but the Cimarrones were a strong-willed and determined people. They escaped slavery and created their own communities in Panamá's jungles so they could maintain their freedom."

"I wish I'd known this stuff before." I look down at my feet. "I could have shared it with my class."

Enrique's words from the other day when we were talking about my presentation replay in my head. I really should have let my parents help me with my project. At that exact moment, I feel Enrique's eyes burning a hole through the side of my face. I look at him just in time to see him mouthing the words *I told you so*. I flare my nostrils and roll my eyes at him.

"Ma, remember the last time we were in Panamá? We had so much fun at Abuela Rosalyn's house," Enrique says.

"We sure did," Ma agrees. "We need to go soon and stay with mi mamá again. Maybe in May, for Etnia Negra."

"What's that?" I ask.

"Every year in May, Panamanian people celebrate their African culture," Pa explains. "There are a bunch of parades and festivals. The students wear traditional African clothes to school. It's kind of like Black History Month here in the States."

"African culture is a huge part of Panamá's history and ours. Even the Diablos Rojos buses you love riding in Panamá. Many Panamanians of West Indian descent painted them." With a firm tone of voice, Ma starts speaking slowly and clearly. "On both sides of the family, we come from the Caribbean. I also always want you to remember we come from Africa first."

EIGHTEEN

~eeee~

What's So Wrong with Having Braids?

Describe the effect of multiplying or dividing a
number by one, by zero, by a number between zero
and one, and by a number greater than one.

WHAT DOES THIS even mean? I've been going through this
five-page math packet for an hour now, trying to remember
when I learned this stuff. Mrs. Taylor handed it out today,
saying we only needed to do our best. She's using this packet
to figure out what to focus on teaching us this year. Math is
not my thing, and even though this packet will not be graded,
I'm still taking my time, doing the best I can. Right now, my
best is just three or four math equations that are halfway
solved on each page. I'm probably going to leave these word
problems blank.

The clock on my phone reads 8:00 p.m. on the dot. That means it's time to be done with homework. This packet isn't due until Friday, so maybe I'll try again tomorrow. Plus, around nine is when Michael and I usually start texting until we get tired.

I gather all my completed homework assignments and slide them into my folder. When I flip the top flap of my school bag open to put my folder away, I see my journal lying sideways between my social studies book and my glitter spiral notebook. The other day I decided to start taking my journal to school with me in case I want to write in it while I'm there. Seeing it now, when I have the rest of tonight completely free, is the push I needed to finally start writing in it again.

I search the word *Panama* online and scroll through all the links until I find something interesting. Holding my favorite pen, my hand starts to shake as it nears the page in my journal. I use my left hand to steady the right one and stop shaking. When it's finally calm, I begin.

~~~~~~

Dear Journal,

This is the first time I've touched these pages since Abuelo died. I want to start writing in here again like I used to. I think I've been kind of scared. Not "I think." I know I have been masking my fear as being too busy dealing with Abuela drama. I kind of felt like writing in my journal meant I was moving on from Abuelo. Now I see that is not true. So here I go. I'm going to start slowly with something easy: my daily "Panamanian facts."

Today's fact is about the Nazareno, or Cristo Negro. He is a life-size statue of Jesus Christ made out of wood that is displayed on an altar in a Catholic church in Portobelo, Panama. Usually, pictures of Jesus show him as a white man with long blond hair. But the Cristo Negro is Black. A crown sits on his thick, coarse hair, and he wears a robe that gets changed twice a year. Over his left shoulder is a dark brown cross. People from faraway places come to see the Cristo Negro to ask for his help.

Wow. A real-life Black Jesus. I never knew this existed. Next time we go to Panama, I'm going to ask Ma and Pa to take me to see Him.

Sincerely,
Sicily

ℓℓℓℓ ℓ ℓℓℓℓ ℓ ℓℓℓ ℓ ℓℓℓℓ ℓ ℓℓℓℓ

For some time now, I've felt like something has been missing or something has fallen off me, and I haven't been able to figure out what it is. But after writing in my journal for the first time in a while, I feel whole. And I know now that writing is what I've been missing.

I flip to a new page so I can write some more. After quickly jotting down what I remember about Bayano from last night's conversation, I decide I want to keep going, filling in every page of my journal. What should I write though? Most people use their journals to write about their feelings or how their day went or the good things that happen to them. Nothing good has happened to me.

Wait. Something good did happen yesterday. After Pa and Ma left my room last night, I realized they didn't ground me for how I treated Abuela at dinner. They probably understood how hurt I was by her, and then we started talking about my class presentation.

Since then, I've been low-key and mostly out of sight.

During dinner this evening, which Abuela was absent from, I kept my mouth shut. Enrique made it easy for me though. He was so excited about making the football team at his school that he broke his usual routine of scarfing down his food and avoiding Pa and Ma's questions. He talked football the whole time we ate.

When Pa or Ma had a chance to ask me anything, I made sure I was as proper and respectful as possible, using "yes ma'am" and "no sir" when necessary. It was probably a bit much, but when it comes to my parents, I never know. A few weeks from now I could be going along having a great day, and *boom*! Out of nowhere, they'll remember they never punished me. I hope that if I act right, maybe they'll continue to let me slide.

It's been almost three hours since dinner, and my stomach is doing that loud, embarrassing growl that it always does when I'm in a quiet room full of people. As I open my bedroom door to head downstairs for a snack, I hear voices talking quietly, almost whispering. I creep down, sliding my back against the wall, trying not to be seen or heard.

When I get to the second-to-last step, I recognize Pa and Abuela's voices. I didn't hear the doorbell. When did she get here? From where I'm standing, I see Pa sitting on the couch with his back toward me and Abuela sitting sort of diagonally across the room from him in the recliner. Both of them are sipping from mugs with steam rising out of them.

Hmm, should I say hello to her? Kind of as a way to say sorry for how I acted without actually having to say the words? And so Pa can see me being nice to her? No, I'll save it for the next time Abuela is here for dinner so Ma can see my fake kindness too.

I hop over the last step and speed to the kitchen, all while praying Abuela's eyes don't catch me. I move around in the darkness, remembering where the table and chairs, trash can, and center island are so I don't bump into them. When I open the refrigerator door, the light bulb shines on my face like a spotlight. I grab a string cheese from one of the middle drawers and let the fridge door close gradually by itself. That's when I hear Pa say my name—not like he's calling me, but like he's talking about me.

I step lightly across the kitchen, and my feet stick to the cold tile floor. Someone needs to mop. I'm not telling Ma though because she'll make that someone be me. Standing by the archway, I cautiously peel open the two plastic flaps of the string cheese wrapper but pull them so fast the cheese pops out, and I have to scramble to catch it before it hits the floor.

"You can't continue saying things like that to her. She's my daughter, your granddaughter," I hear Pa say. Even though he has a drink, his voice sounds dry, like it hurts him to speak. "What's going on with you lately? Ever since the doctor increased your arthritis medication, you've been acting differently."

"Ay, por favor. The medicine doesn't have any side effects. I am fine," Abuela says.

"You still haven't told me, Mamá. What's so wrong with having braids?" Pa asks.

"I don't like Sicily looking like that."

"Enrique walks around here with an unkempt Afro. Some days it's lopsided, others it has lint in it and smells of that stinky spray that he uses. I want to grab him, put him in the car, and drive him straight to the barbershop," Pa says.

"Yes, do it!" I shout whisper. *Shoot.* I slap my palm over my mouth, which makes a slight clap noise. The living room gets quiet.

Double shoot. I'm about to get caught. I fight the urge to run up to my room and stay put as they go back to talking.

"Oh, Enrique looks fine. Let him be," Abuela says.

Really. I pull off a piece of cheese from the stick and let it sit in my mouth. Abuela hates my braids, yet she's cool with Enrique's messy fro? I shake my head. I am so glad I didn't say hello when I came downstairs. She doesn't deserve it.

"That's exactly what I'm doing—letting him be. He likes his hair that way, and I know it's a popular style right now. So instead of calling him names or mentioning how much I don't like his hair every time I see him, I leave him alone. That's what you need to do when you see Sicily."

"It's not the same," Abuela says.

"How?" Pa asks as I mouth the same question. "They are

both allowed to wear their hair how they want. Neither of them is hurting anyone, so I don't see the big deal."

"Things are different for girls."

"What are you talking about?"

"I just don't like the way braids look." Abuela's voice gets louder.

"¿Por qué? Why?" Pa asks.

"Braiding Sicily's hair was fine when she was little, but she's growing up now. She needs to stop putting in that fake hair. It's not acceptable."

"Acceptable to who?"

Beep.

The refrigerator alarm goes off, alerting that the door is not completely shut. I hear movement that sounds like Pa has gotten up from the couch. I take a step back, out of the archway, then tiptoe run over to the door and push it closed. *Pleeeease don't let them have heard that.*

"Where I grew up in Panamá, people never wore braids. I never saw that style until I was an adult, traveling to Panamá City for work. And even then, only the girls in the poor neighborhoods wore their hair like that. The rest of us relaxed our hair and looked professional. I remember working at a store in Panamá. Although it wasn't against the law to wear your hair natural or in braids, supervisors often asked employees to straighten their hair. If they didn't, they got placed in the back of the store so customers wouldn't see them."

"Things are different now." I walk back over to the archway and stick my head out of the kitchen, as far as possible without moving my body. I see Pa walking back and forth, just as he did in my room last night, and twisting his wedding ring around his finger.

"You may not like it, but that's just how things are," Abuela says. "Appearance matters. The way you look can help you in your career. I just want the best for Sicily."

By calling me names?

"You're not getting it." Pa sits, and his voice becomes stiff. I hear him take a deep breath. "You've made silly comments about Sicily's braids in the past, and I paid it no attention. That all changed the other day. You really hurt her feelings. I've never seen Sicily so upset and bothered by something someone said to her. Never."

"Oh, it wasn't that bad. She can handle it. My parents used to say worse to me. Kids are too sensitive these days," Abuela says, waving her hand like she's shooing a fly away. "You both need to stop babying her."

What? They don't baby me!

"You're wrong. Sicily has been walking around here for days feeling bad. And as her father, I feel terrible because *my* mother is the one who hurt her. I don't want Sicily to feel self-conscious about the way she looks. A few years ago, we had a tough time getting her to accept her widow's peak."

I cover my mouth and giggle. I used to complain about

my hairline all the time. I hated how it came to a letter V at the top of my forehead. I wanted a perfect hairline like Ma's. Ma would always tell me there is no such thing as perfect, and anything different about me is what makes me, me.

"Since then, Carmen and I have made it a priority to make sure Sicily is confident in who she is and confident about the way she looks. I want her to always feel beautiful just the way she is."

Aw, Pa. I stick more cheese into my mouth and smile.

"Wait a minute—" Abuela starts to say.

"Listen to me," Pa cuts her off. By his tone of voice, I can tell he has had enough of this. "This world is very harsh to Black women, and you know that. At some point in Sicily's life, people will speak negatively about her simply because of the color of her skin or her features. The last thing I want is for her to have to deal with that here at home." Pa stops talking, and I hear him take a gulp from his mug.

I know what Pa is saying is true because it's already happened. In kindergarten, this girl's mom and little brother came to visit our class. Her little brother kept staring at me and then asked his mom why my skin was so dark. I felt like something was wrong with me. And being the only Black person in the class didn't help. That night, I asked Ma why Pa and Enrique are the color of the light brown crayon and why she and I are the color of the dark brown crayon. She said there are many different shades of Black skin, and one is not better or worse than the other.

I tilt my head toward the living room with more string cheese hanging from my mouth, waiting to hear Abuela say she understands and is sorry for what she said to me. But no. There's only the sound of someone—who I know is Abuela—slurping liquid. She always makes that noise when she drinks something hot.

I can tell Pa is trying his hardest to get Abuela to see his point. For whatever reason, she won't do it. Doesn't she understand that styles change? Just because people didn't wear braids or braids with extensions when she was younger doesn't mean it's wrong.

"Aren't you at least worried about how this is affecting your relationship with her? You two used to be so close. Are you willing to give that up?" Pa asks Abuela.

The room is silent. So silent, I hold my breath out of fear Pa and Abuela might hear it.

"¿Nada?" Pa asks her. "You have nothing to say?"

"I don't know what you want me to say." Abuela sounds like she is annoyed.

"Mamá, I love you very much. I put up with a lot that goes on between you and Carmen, but this is where I have to draw the line. I can't allow you to keep coming over here and speaking to Sicily like that. So the choice is yours. Stop talking to Sicily about her hair, or you aren't welcomed here anymore."

I gasp and suck in all the air around me. I've wished for this to happen, but I'm still shocked that Pa actually did it.

"Well," Abuela says. I imagine her sitting there, trying to grip the cross on her necklace in her palm.

Next, I hear keys jingling and feet shuffling. I walk quietly to the farthest corner of the kitchen, slide down against the wall to the floor, and hold my breath.

"I guess I have some things to think about," I hear Abuela say.

I hear their footsteps heading toward the front door, so I creep back over to where I was and continue listening. The lock clicks and the wooden front door creaks open.

"I remember you used to always say that our tongue has the power to speak life or death into a situation or person. Think about what your words are doing to Sicily," Pa says. Then the door closes and he goes upstairs.

I can't believe Abuela. She wants me to stop wearing braids so badly that she's no longer willing to see her family? No longer willing to talk to me anymore? Maybe I had this whole thing wrong. I thought my relationship with Abuela was special, important. If she has to go home and think about things, I guess that means she never saw us the way I did.

NINETEEN

Ideas

Fr: Marconi@Chisholm.edu
Bcc: SicilyJordan@eMail.com
Subject: Chisholm Is Talking Writing Session

Hey all,

I hope your submissions are coming along nicely. Remember, they are due next week. Erin Masterson has suggested another meeting so everyone can have time to work on their submissions.

I spoke to the school librarian, and she has reserved some tables for us to use on Wednesday for two hours after school. I encourage you to come prepared with any questions or concerns or just show up and write.

The bell rings and we all rush out the classroom door as if Mrs. Taylor had been holding us hostage all day. Reyna and I usually head to the courtyard after school and meet up with Kiara and Kamaya before walking home. Only today, Reyna stays behind to speak with Mrs. Taylor. I have no idea what they're going to talk about, but I'm thankful for the chance to slip away.

Reyna would be pissed if she knew I was going to meet her cousin. Well, technically, I'm going to see him at the magazine meeting. Whatever the case, I know by the way Reyna bashes Michael every chance she gets that she would not be cool with me hanging out with him. Or texting him. Or worse, liking him. I have to keep all of this to myself. Reyna and I are BFFs again. I can't ruin that.

I speed-walk straight through the middle of campus like I'm late for something. Even though we texted last night, I haven't seen Michael since Monday at lunch. It's been way too long.

When I'm close to the library, I slow my pace. At the big windows near the library's entrance, I stop myself from looking at my reflection. I don't know who might be on the other side of the windows, and the last thing I want is for someone to see me fixing myself up. Super embarrassing.

I walk into the library and spot Mr. Marconi sitting at one of the tables, reading a thick book. He looks up, waves, and smiles, then goes back to reading. Michael told me he was coming. Other than the few people I recognize from the first meeting, the library is pretty empty. *I hope Michael didn't change his mind.* I sit at one of the reserved tables just as Mr. Marconi stands to speak.

"Okay, guys. I'll be here reading my book until 4:00 p.m.," he says, after sipping from his *Life without algebra is boring* water bottle. "If you have any questions, come on over. If not, use this time to work on your submissions. I'm sure more people are on their way, so please remember to keep your voices down."

I pull out my glitter spiral notebook and my journal from my school bag and take out my phone to do a little more research on Portobelo for today's journal fact. Since it's technically after school, I shouldn't get in trouble for having it out.

~~~~~~~~~~~~~~~~~~~~~~~~~~~~~~~

Dear Journal,

Today's fact is about a place in Panama called Portobelo. This place was a major port for slave ships. I can't imagine what it must have been like to be taken from the only home you'd ever known, put on a ship, have no idea where you are being taken to, and then end up enslaved.

Before the Panama Canal was built, ships carrying goods docked on Panama's Atlantic side, and slaves had to unload goods and then transport them by land (across Panama) to the Pacific, where they then had to reload the goods onto another ship. While doing this, many slaves escaped into the forests of Panama. These are the escaped slaves, called Cimarrones, who Ma talked about the other night.

Sincerely,
Sicily

ℓℓℓℓ ℓ ℓℓℓℓ ℓℓℓℓ ℓ ℓℓℓℓ

I wish I could use all the stuff I've been writing in my journal about Panamá for my magazine submission. But I can't do that. It would just end up being a report about a country, which is something I know no one wants to read in the school's online magazine.

I slide my journal back into my bag. I turn to the page in my spiral notebook that has the list I've been making of possible submission topics.

- Why we need a school student store
- School spirit day ideas
- Halloween costumes and party ideas

High-pitched laughter breaks the silence in the library. "You are too funny!"

I stop writing and look up to see Michael and a thirsty Erin Masterson walking into the library. She has her arm hooked around his while both of his hands are in his pockets.

You would think Michael is a famous comedian by how loud Erin Masterson is laughing. It's so obvious that she wants everyone to see she is with him. After the librarian shushes her, Erin Masterson puts her hand over her mouth and continues giggling.

She pulls Michael toward the table where her two friends are sitting. I watch Michael sit with them, and my arm suddenly feels like I'm at the doctor's office and a nurse is pushing a long, thin needle into it. I rub at the would-be injection spot, lower my head, and go back to writing my list. Even though I have no more ideas, I pretend I'm busy, so I don't have to watch *her* flirt with him. If I could, my magazine submission would be a top ten list of all the annoying students at this school, and Erin Masterson would be number one.

"Ha ha!" I giggle to myself, still looking down at my notebook.

"Wassup?"

I flinch as Michael sits down across from me. *Thump. Thump. Thump. Thump.* My heart starts beating out of control. My mouth falls slightly open, and my cheeks become hot. I start fidgeting with one of my braids so my hands will stop shaking.

"What's so funny?" he asks.

"Oh, I was just thinking about a joke I heard earlier."

"Tell me."

"Oh . . . it-it was nothing," I say. I don't know why I'm nervous about him sitting here with me. It's like I'm breaking some kind of rule or something.

"Your necklace." Michael stands up and leans across the table toward me. He reaches his hand out and lifts the nameplate on my necklace. "This font is so cool. Where did you get this from?"

"Thanks." I look down at it. "My mom had it made in Panamá. I've had it since I was a baby."

When I look up, our eyes connect, and I quickly look back down at his hand, holding my name in his palm. *He's so cute.*

"For a long time," I continue, "I thought the font was just a random choice my mom made when she ordered it. Then one time in Panamá, I noticed that a lot of Panamanians with nameplates have the same font. It's like we belong to a cool secret club or something."

We both laugh louder than we should in the library.

"Ssshhhhhhh!"

I look over to the other table. Erin Masterson has her finger up to her mouth as her friends stare me down.

"So, you hang out with her?" I whisper to Michael.

"I was walking over when she grabbed my arm. She talked my ear off the whole way here," he says, messing with his Philippines wristband. "Oh, I forgot to tell you. I spoke to Mr. Marconi, and he's going to let me take pictures for the magazine. I'm here to find out what people are writing about and see what pics they need for their submissions," Michael says, smiling.

"That's a good idea. A picture will go perfectly with some of the topics I'm thinking of writing about."

"What have you come up with?" he asks.

I slide my notebook across the table to him, and our hands touch when he reaches for it. I stare at my hand as a warm, tingly feeling slowly spreads from my fingertips to the rest of my body. From the corner of my eye, I can see Erin Masterson whispering to her friends while looking at me. When I turn my head to look at her, she flips her long blonde ponytail and rolls her eyes.

"This is all I've come up with so far. But I'm not sure if I want to write about any of it," I tell him. I wish I could figure out why coming up with a topic is so hard. Am I putting too much pressure on myself because I want to get picked so badly and prove that I really do have the gift? Or is it because

I want to beat Erin Masterson? I just know my topic has to be something major, something to get everyone's attention, and these ideas I have written down are not it.

"You always look good in your uniform and that day you came over last weekend. Why don't you write about clothes or the cool stuff you wear?"

My cheeks become hot again. I look up at him and smile.

"Remember the first meeting? All the other girls said they want to write about fashion. I want to do something different." I grab my phone to find a recent article I read on *Teen Vogue*'s site and show Michael. "If I were to write anything about clothes or accessories, I would do it like this."

Michael comes over to my side of the table and sits in the chair next to me. I hold my phone between us. He scoots his chair closer to me—so close I can see the hairs at the corner of his mouth.

I show him an article about a clothing designer who makes shoes with recycled materials and gives them to children in need. And another article about a fifteen-year-old who creates T-shirts and donates the profits to causes and organizations in struggling countries.

"I guess this is fashion but covered in a different way."

"These are pretty cool articles. I didn't know these kinds of magazines talked about this stuff," Michael says.

"I know, right? I would love to write for them one day. They always have really good articles."

"It's cool that you're into writing," he says. "Why do you do it?"

"I don't really know how to explain it. Probably because nobody has ever asked me that," I say. "I know it's always been a part of me, you know? I love sitting with paper, a pen, and my thoughts and just writing. It's like a freeing feeling that lets me leave this world for a little bit and be a part of a new one, one that I create."

I pause and squeeze my eyes shut. *Did I say too much? Does he think I'm weird?* When I open my eyes and look at him, he's leaning toward me a little, staring like he is hanging on to my every word.

Instead of saying writing is boring, like Reyna did, or should be my hobby, like my parents, Michael just listens to me. And that gives me a push, a feeling that I can do anything I've ever wanted to do. It's kind of like how talks with Abuela used to make me feel.

"So do you have a site where you post your writing?" he asks.

"No, right now I just write in my journal."

"That's what's up," he says, nodding.

"Psst, Michael." Erin Masterson motions him toward her and pats the seat of the chair next to her. Michael shakes his head and continues looking at the article on my phone.

"Man, she bugs," he whispers to me.

"Yeah, she *does*."

Once again, Erin Masterson is staring me down from her table while twirling her hair around her finger. Then she gets up and heads straight over to us.

"I don't know why you're here," Erin Masterson says, standing next to me. She's wearing a pin that says, *Positive Vibes Only.* "I had my father speak to Mr. Marconi this morning, and they agreed." She bends down closer to me. "Eighth graders only."

A chill comes over me, and I instantly start cracking my knuckles. I'm ready to stand up so I can be face-to-face with her, just like Reyna was the other day in the courtyard.

"Stop lying," Michael says. "You know I'm in seventh grade, and you keep telling me how important it is that I write for the magazine."

Erin Masterson walks over to Michael and puts her hand on his shoulder. "You're different," she tells him, looking over at me. I lock my eyes on hers. If she wants a staring contest, she's got it. Enrique and I used to do this all the time, and I always won, so I have no problem staring at her ice-colored eyes all day long. When she sees I'm not backing down, she turns to walk away so fast her hair swishes as it flies through the air.

"I swear she acts just like Reyna," Michael says.

"Really? How?" I say. "They seem nothing alike to me."

"Reyna is so bossy and thinks she's in charge of everyone and everything at home." A vein pops out on the side of

Michael's neck as he leans back in the chair and crosses his arms.

"Oh." I pick at my nail polish.

"And she has the worst attitude. Sometimes she'll just snap at me for no reason," he adds. "I try to avoid her most of the time and hang out with her sister, Maria. She's pretty chill."

Not knowing what to say, I stay silent and stare straight ahead. I've never seen that side of Reyna before. She's been nothing but nice to me and stood up to Erin Masterson for me.

"Soooo, do you have a camera?" I ask. "Or are you going to borrow one from the school lab?"

"Reyna thinks she's so funny too." Michael keeps going like he's been waiting to let all of this out. I just wish he weren't telling me. Yes, he's talking about his cousin. He's *also* talking about my BFF. "The other day, I was telling my aunt how much I miss my parents and my little sister. Reyna overheard and has been making fun of me about it ever since."

I clear my throat and scratch the side of my face with my pointer finger. I don't know what Michael expects me to say. I do know I can never, ever come clean to Reyna about my kind of, sort of crush on her cousin. She would probably end up hating me as much as she hates him. Or hate me as much as he hates her. *Ugh. This is too much.*

"And Reyna loves to latch on to stuff you say and never let

it go," he says. "Sometimes I wish I had moved to the Philippines with my family."

His face looks expressionless, like stone. He's not even blinking, just staring down at the table. It's messed up that Reyna is teasing him like that. Instead of saying that to him, I reach out and put my hand on his back.

Not saying anything to defend Reyna makes me feel like I'm a horrible friend. I mean, am I supposed to tell Reyna about this? Should I tell her to leave Michael alone because it's not funny? Or do I ask him to stop talking about my friend? Or should I tell them both that they feel the same exact way about each other?

I feel trapped, stuck in the middle of something, and I have no idea how I got here. I turn to Michael. He is still in a daze, like his mind is somewhere else, and I feel sorry for him. The longest I've ever been away from my family was for a week when I went to church camp. I can't imagine what it feels like to be in a different country, away from close family.

As for Michael and Reyna, I'm keeping my mouth shut and out of their drama.

TWENTY

Race and Culture

"HEY, PA." I close the car door and buckle my seatbelt. When I texted him and Ma to let them know I was about to start walking home after the magazine writing session, Pa wrote back and said he'd pick me up.

"Did you get out early again?" I ask him.

"Yes, I have a ten-page paper to write, and it's due tomorrow night."

"Ooohhhh, I'm tellllllinnnggg!" I sing while shaking my finger at him. "You're not supposed to wait until the last minute to do your homework."

Along with being in the military, Pa is also one semester away from getting his criminal justice degree. He has classes on Tuesday and Thursday nights at San Diego State University.

Pa laughs. "Okay, you got me. You make sure you do as I

175

say and not as I do," he tells me. "I'm going to the library. Do you want to come with me?"

Even though I just came from a library, I nod my head yes. The downtown library is one of my favorite places. It's huge compared to the one at school. And on weekends, there is always an event on the lawn out front or something new to see inside.

After parking the car, we walk into the library lobby, and it smells like someone has sprayed air freshener that smells like bleach. *Yuck.* I hate that smell. My body shivers as I walk past the yellow Caution Wet Floor sign. Pa and I stand in front of the wall-mounted fish tank and watch the tropical fish swim around. The last time I was here, the tank only had a bunch of starfish that just sat at the bottom. These new bright fish make the whole library entrance come alive.

"I'm going up to the second floor to work at a private desk," Pa says. "Come check in with me in an hour."

"Okay, Pa," I say as the escalator takes him upstairs. I should go up there with him and work on my magazine submission. Instead, I head to the youth section.

None of the books on the New to the Library table look interesting, so I walk through a few stacks. Again, none of the titles catch my attention, probably because it's hard to focus on anything. The section is full of crying babies and a bunch of loud little kids. Their parents must have forgotten that a library is a place where you are supposed to be quiet.

I venture out to the library's main area. Even though it's packed with people, they are working at tables, reading on couches, and looking through the stacks, so this area is much quieter.

On my way to find a couch to chill on, I walk past the computer lab and remember my social studies homework. Today, Mrs. Taylor assigned another timeline for us to complete, this time for 1862, the second year of the American Civil War. I speed-walk into the lab and grab the only computer station available.

Sitting on the stool, I think about when I was working on the first timeline and how curious I was about the way Black people were treated in Panamá back in the day. So instead of searching for information to fill in my second timeline, I pull up the library's information system home page and type *slavery in Panama* in the search box. Over a hundred pages of results come up. There are links to all kinds of information on the subject. I click on Images at the top of the page and see many black-and-white photos.

A map of Africa and North, Central, and South America covered with red arrows catches my eye. The title is "Slave Trade from Africa to the Americas." When I click to enlarge it, I see Africa's left side is labeled "West African Slave Trade Region." Each red arrow starts at a different country in West Africa and stretches out to other countries across the Atlantic Ocean. The arrow pointing to Panamá has the number

0.2 million next to it. The map tells me this is the number of African people brought to Panamá as slaves. I pull my journal and pen out from my school bag and start noting important facts.

This map makes it pretty easy to understand how and why Black people are in Latin American countries. I pull my phone out of my pocket, hold it up to the computer screen, and snap a picture of the map. If anyone else ever questions me about Black people and Panamá, I'm showing them this picture.

I put my phone down next to the computer and start reading through different articles. *Afro-colonial* comes up a lot in the search results, so I click on one and learn that *Afro-colonial* is the term used for Panamanians who are descendants of slaves. The article goes on to list a whole bunch of facts that I never knew. Like, the first Black slaves started arriving in Panamá in the early 1500s, with explorers Governor Diego de Nicuesa and Vasco Núñez de Balboa.

I know him.

Well, not really. We drive by his statue almost every day when we're in Panamá. I've seen it so many times, looking out toward the ocean, and never knew anything about him. This article says he is credited with discovering the Pacific Ocean, but that the Indigenous people of Panamá had already been living there and knew of the Pacific as early as 12,000 BC.

Hmm. So this guy was basically another Christopher Columbus.

The next article says that slaves taken to Panamá were often sold in Panamá and to nearby countries. The article also mentions Bayano's rebellion. Since Pa and Ma talked about him the other night, I skip over that part.

It's crazy how this relates to what I'm learning in social studies about the Civil War. I hate that Black people were thought of as nothing more than free labor, not only here in the United States but also pretty much everywhere else.

Next I type *Black people in Panama* in the search box. Again, pages and pages of results load on the screen. The first picture I see when I click Images shows Black men working around white boxes. When I click the image to make it bigger, the photo description appears: "Caribbean workers, known as 'Powder Men,' working with dynamite to blast through rock." It goes on to say this was the most dangerous job to have as a Panamá Canal worker because many of the Powder Men were injured or died in explosions.

I wonder if anyone in my family was a Powder Man.

I click back to the search results and find a website that estimates 200,000 people from the West Indies, mostly from Barbados and Jamaica, moved to Panamá for work. They started arriving in the 1850s to work on the railroad. They continued coming in the years that followed to work on the canal. Black canal workers experienced a lot of racial discrimination, and it affected how much they got paid.

Canal workers from the United States were known as "gold" employees, and West Indian workers were known as "silver." Silver employees were paid less than gold employees, and areas around town were labeled to keep silver and gold workers apart. Silver employees were separated just like Black people were here in the United States. The difference was that instead of signs reading "Whites Only," Panamanian signs read "Gold," and instead of signs reading "Colored," Panamanian signs read "Silver."

It's impossible to ignore that this policy was about race, not ethnicity, because canal authorities tried their best to categorize the few African American workers who arrived as silver employees rather than gold. A limited number of African American workers were able to keep their gold status, but it often did little to protect them. As a result, there was never a large population of African American canal workers. Even though I'm not surprised, I'm still in disbelief.

As if the discrimination weren't enough, the work conditions were terrible. Workers had to do backbreaking labor in bad weather. Worst of all, mosquitos carried and spread diseases like malaria and yellow fever. Many canal workers died from the outbreak. By 1914, when the 48-mile-long canal was completed, 25,000 workers had died because of something work-related.

All the times I've visited and seen ships pass through the Panamá Canal, I never knew or even thought about all that went into building it. *Twenty-five thousand workers* is the only thought that echoes in my mind.

My phone vibrates, making a loud buzzing sound on the wooden table.

Reyna Sado
What u doin?

Sicily Jordan
At the library

Reyna Sado
AGAIN!!! BOOOO! LOLOLOL!

Ha ha, Reyna is a mess. After taking off my dangling heart earrings, I put on the headphones plugged into the computer and click Play on a one-minute, thirty-five-second video.

Many workers moved from various West Indian countries to build the Panamá Canal. They lived there for years, and Panamá became their new home. Workers got married and had children, all while adapting to Panamanian culture. Yet the workers still embraced the cultures they came from. This was evident in the food they ate, their accents, and their traditions. This is why many Panamanians follow West Indian traditions, and those same traditions can be traced to Africa.

These canal workers moved to Panamá, and despite adjusting to Panamanian culture, they were still Black first. This is what happened in my family. Ma and Pa were born in Panamá, and they are Black. Enrique and I were born in the United States, and we are Black too. The country you are born in has nothing to do with your race. The difference is culture. Enrique and I have a mix of all three—African and West Indian cultures from our ancestors, Panamanian culture from Pa and Ma, and American culture because this is where we live. Something clicks in my brain. Race and culture—this is what Enrique was talking about before.

This is amazing: to sit here, looking at images of *my* people and learning that they migrated from one country to another for more opportunities and dealt with harsh treatment while building a canal that is one of the wonders of the modern world. Like, I come from a line of strong-willed people. Strong-willed *Black* people.

My hour is almost up, and I have to check in with Pa before he gets mad at me. When I stand up, my chest rises and fills with air. I close my eyes for a second and take in what I'm feeling at this moment. Learning new things about who I am and where I come from has awakened something inside of me, and I know I am forever changed.

TWENTY-ONE

Up All Night

I'M SO GLAD it's Friday because Ma is letting me have a sleepover tonight. I invited everyone: Reyna, the Tether Squad, and Kamaya and Kiara. But Reyna and Evelyn are the only ones who got permission to come this time around. Even though they won't be here until later, I start cleaning up my room as soon as I get home from school. I know if I don't do it now, Ma will make me do it when she gets home from work.

While making up my bed, I think about all the fun we're going to have tonight. It's cool that my two friends get to meet each other. I know Reyna is going to love Evelyn's jokes, and Evelyn is going to love Reyna's style.

Only . . . what if they don't get along? I bite my bottom lip. I mean, Reyna is chill and calm, like me. Evelyn, on the other hand . . . She can be *a lot* for some people, even if those people's opinions are 100 percent *wrong*. Ugh, I hope this all works out.

I push the negative thought out of my head and get back to cleaning my room. I need to hurry because after I finish, I'm taking my braids out and washing my hair in the kitchen sink. Evelyn promised to do my hair tonight. I swear, that girl has been braiding since she was born. She, her mom, and her three older sisters all know how. Braiding skills just run in her family. I bet her little brother can braid too.

While straightening up the books on my desk and putting pens and papers into the drawers, I remember I haven't written in my journal today. So I stop cleaning, sit at my desk, and do some research online.

Dear Journal,

Today's fact: Congo dance of Panama. There's actually more than one dance. They've been passed down for many years. Everything I read said the dances are "the most unique and colorful manifestation of folklore in the province of Colón, Panama." I'm not sure exactly what that means. I also watched a few videos on YouTube and saw that the women wear really pretty colorful blouses and skirts, flowers in their hair, and no shoes. The men wear fringed shirts and pants made of out of colored material, and they also don't wear shoes. To the beat of drums and singing, these Congo dancers act out the stories of struggle and hurt that the Cimarrones felt during slavery in Panama.

Sincerely,
Sicily

When I'm done with my journal entry, I start hanging my clean clothes in the closet.

"Hey, loser!" Enrique says, bursting into my room.

"What do you want?"

"I heard you're having a sleepover tonight," he says, lying on my bed. "What are you guys gonna do? Talk about boys?"

"Oh my gosh, shut up!" *Shoot.* My pollera. Even though my laundry basket is on the opposite side of the closet, I slide the other door closed, just in case.

"So I guess that means yes, you guys *are* gonna talk about boys. *Whack!* After I empty the trash and vacuum, I'm outta here. I'm going to spend the night at Rashaan's house."

"Oh, are you guys gonna talk about girls?" I ask.

"No, we're grown men. We don't talk about them. We hang out with them."

"Ew, girls actually *like* you?"

"Hey, I'm a very handsome guy," he says, sitting up and dusting his shoulder off.

"Lies you tell." Our laughing is interrupted by the front door closing downstairs.

"Uh-oh, Ma's home, and I haven't even started my chores." Enrique gets up and runs out of my room so fast that he almost trips.

I finish hanging up my clothes, and then I dig through my dresser drawers for pajamas to wear tonight. I narrow my choices down to two options: dark blue shorts and a matching tank top or my simple gray sweatpants and a big T-shirt. I stand next to my bed, staring down at my two choices laid out in front of me.

"What are you doing?" Ma asks from my bedroom door.

"Trying to pick out PJs for tonight."

"Shouldn't you just worry about being comfortable?"

"Really, Ma?" I ask.

She shakes her head. "Let me know when I should order the pizza. And I bought some soda, chips, and cookies. That should be enough, right?"

"Yeah, that's fine. Thanks, Ma."

With mouths full of pizza, Reyna, Evelyn, and I laugh non-stop all night. The muscles in my cheeks hurt along with my head. When Evelyn braided my hair earlier, I quickly learned that she is more heavy-handed than Ma. It felt like she was

186

pulling the life out of my body through my scalp. Her fingers gripped and pulled my hair back so tightly I can hardly squeeze my eyes shut now.

That doesn't matter though because Evelyn slayed my hair. I can't wait until I'm as good as she is. She did medium-sized cornrows, each starting at my hairline and meeting in the middle of my head. And then she twisted the long braids into a cute top-knot bun. This style should last me at least two weeks.

Hours later, my head still tingles as Reyna and I crack up laughing at Evelyn, who is doing impressions of people. Since the day I met her on the tetherball court, Evelyn has *always* cracked me up. She's so extra and I love it. I think Evelyn should be a comedian, but she wants to be an actress. Last year, she watched an old seventies movie with her grandma called *Mahogany*. After learning that the word is used to describe Black people, Evelyn told everyone they needed to use *mahogany* when describing her. She even tells people it's her middle name, ha ha!

I wipe a single tear from my cheek and hold my stomach when Evelyn offers to come to Chisholm to beat up Erin Masterson.

"For real, I'll do it," she says. Evelyn jumps up from the floor where we are sitting and starts kicking and punching the air, all while laughing and telling us how serious she is.

"Ev, you couldn't hurt a fly," I say once I catch my breath. "Erin Masterson's not worth it."

"Right, she just needs someone to check her real good," Reyna says. "And if she says anything to Sicily or me again, I'll be the one to do it."

Reyna gets up from the floor and walks around, picking things up and touching stuff, just like I did last weekend in her room.

"How come you never wear this?" she asks, holding up my necklace with a Panamá map pendant on it.

"I don't know. I like this one better," I say, touching my nameplate on my chest.

"Yo, I love that your family is from Panama," Evelyn says. "I wish my family was from somewhere."

"What do you mean? Everyone's family comes from somewhere," Reyna says.

"Yeah, Birmingham, Alabama. Before that, I think West Africa. I don't know anything more than that," Evelyn says, shrugging her shoulders. "Where's your family from?"

"The Philippines," Reyna says. "I'm like Sicily, first-generation American."

"See. I think that is so cool, you guys," Evelyn says. "Sicily, I remember your tenth birthday party when your mom made that purple-ish red drink for us to try. Remember? It had like a dry, sweet taste."

"Sorrel," I say. "You remember that?"

"Yes, it was good."

"*Yuck*, I hate it. I'll call you the next time my mom makes it." I laugh.

"What about the rapper Noreaga? I heard he's from Panama," Reyna says.

"No, I think he's Puerto Rican. He got his name from the *real* Noriega," I say. As soon as those words leave my mouth, Reyna and Evelyn lean in toward me, all dramatic-like.

"Who's the real one?" they ask.

I lean forward too. Our heads are almost touching. "I don't know much about him," I whisper, adding to the drama. "Except, he was a drug trafficker. The US military invaded Panamá in 1989 just to get him out. A lot of Panamanians hated him after he took control of the military and became a dictator," I say, thinking back to what Ma and Pa told me about him a few years ago.

The corners of my mouth move slightly upward. It feels good being able to answer their questions.

"Wow. You see what I mean?" Evelyn says. "You know about your people. You both know where you come from."

After my trip to the library the other day, I can finally say I do. I do know about my people. I also know exactly how Evelyn's feeling, so I reach my arm out and pat her shoulder.

Evelyn shifts the conversation to clothes and how happy she is that Ravenwood students don't have to wear uniforms. At around 2:00 a.m., the pizza box is empty except for a few pieces of crust. The cookie tray and chip bags are half-empty, and we are lying on the floor in a circle with our heads touching in the middle.

My eyes are heavy, and I've already yawned like a million times when Evelyn brings up the subject of boys.

"What are the boys like at Chisholm?" she asks.

"They're cool, I guess," Reyna says. "What about at Ravenwood?"

"They are bomb! I'll show you some," Evelyn says, reaching for her phone. "This is Brian. He's new, moved here during the summer. And this is Joe. He's in eighth grade."

"And who is this?" Reyna says, snatching Evelyn's phone from her.

"Be careful. That's Shawn. Don't tap any of his pictures. His girlfriend, Lizette, has already tried to fight two girls this week because they liked his pictures. I don't wanna have to beat her up on Monday."

I break my silence and let out a hard laugh as the girls continue scrolling.

"I can see why she acts like that. He is bae," Reyna says.

I watch Reyna and Evelyn through tired, heavy eyes as they pass the phone back and forth. It's almost 2:30 a.m., and I'm ready to sleep.

"I can't believe there are no cute boys at your guys' school. That sucks," Evelyn says. "Oh, wait." Evelyn's head turns my way.

Please no. Please don't bring him up.

"Sicily, you told me about some guy you thought was cute," Evelyn says.

"Really? You haven't told me about anyone," Reyna says. With both their eyes on me, I feel trapped in some kind of invisible cage.

I let out a fake yawn and mumble, "I don't know." Crawling to my bed, I bust free from the cage and their intense stares.

"Remember? I think his name was Andrew. No, something with an *M*, I think. Marcus or Matthew? Hmm. Whose name starts with an *M*?" Evelyn asks, tapping her chin.

I shrug my shoulders and tie my headscarf over my braids. From the corner of my eye, I see Reyna's left eyebrow slowly rise. It's basically shouting *liar* at me. Has Reyna guessed the name that starts with *M*? If so, has it clicked in her mind that the Michael Evelyn wants me to talk about is her cousin Michael?

Please don't ask me anything, Reyna. Please.

I should have told Evelyn that Michael was a secret, but I never thought it would come up between these two. I prop my pillows up and gently place my head down, trying to get as comfortable as possible as my head starts throbbing from my tight braids. I pull my blanket to my chin and pray for it to be a barrier or some kind of protection from this conversation.

Everyone is quiet as I close my eyes and feel relief when Evelyn moves on to Reyna.

"What about you, girl?"

"I did kind of meet this cute boy at the park by my house the other day. Well, we didn't actually meet. He only said hi," Reyna says. My body perks up, and my eyes pop open. She never told me this.

Chill. You're keeping something from her too.

Evelyn moves closer to Reyna, "Tell me all about him."

Suddenly I feel left out. I mean, I could join this conversation right now if I wanted to. I could come clean to Reyna and talk all night about Michael. *No. I can't.* I can't risk losing my bestie over a boy—a cute boy who is so sweet and nice. And makes me laugh.

"Next time you see him, are you gonna talk to him?" Evelyn asks Reyna.

"No!" Reyna says quickly.

"Uh-oh, what happened?" Evelyn asks.

"Nothing. It's just—" I stare at Reyna. She's tracing the lines in the palm of her hand. "I had a boyfriend last year. We held hands once, and that was it," Reyna admits. "No biggie."

Evelyn goes on to coach Reyna, and I close my eyes again. I hear bits and pieces of things—like flip your hair when he's around, giggle at his jokes, and follow his page—before I fall asleep.

TWENTY-TWO

Una Fiesta

"TIME TO GET up, Sicily," Ma shouts, poking her head into my bedroom. "We're leaving soon."

I sit at the edge of my bed, completely out of it. My head is still a little sore from my fresh braids, and my headscarf is halfway falling off. The clock on my phone reads 1:00 p.m. I've slept the whole morning away.

Well, not entirely. Evelyn left around eight, then Reyna and I cleaned up my room. She left around ten, and I must have crashed right after because I don't remember anything after hearing her say, "Bye."

I wish I'd stayed up because I'm starving and I know I missed Pa's Saturday morning breakfast, hojaldras. They're a welcome change from the oatmeal or cereal Enrique and I usually eat before school.

And just like it has for the past few mornings, my mind automatically wanders to my magazine submission. I still have no idea what to write about. Usually, when I can't figure things out, the first person I talk to is Abuela. But that's a no-go. I'm not asking her for anything, ever. I wish Abuelo were here though. He would have given me a million ideas, and by now, I would already know what to write about.

I reach for my phone. There are a few notifications and a text from Michael.

Michael Sado

> Ur sleepover must have been wild, LOL. Reyna came in this morning lookin like she needed to sleep for a week. R U free today?? Wanna meet up 2 talk about pics for ur submission??

Sicily Jordan

> Yeah, pretty wild, LOL! We didnt go 2 sleep until early this morning. I cant meet up with u today, I have a family thing to go to. Lets try 2 meet up another day.

Michael Sado

> ok

Sicily Jordan

> What about u? What r u doing today?

"Hey, let me borrow your charger. I can't find mine," Enrique yells from down the hall.

"Come get it!" I shout back.

"You could have thrown it down the hall to me," he says, walking into my room.

"I need your help with something," I say.

"No! Last time you asked for my help, you had me here for twenty minutes while you tried to figure out what to wear to the park." He shakes his head. "The park!"

"I already picked out what I'm wearing today. See?" I say, pointing to the clothes laid out on my bed. "My ripped blue jeans and white *IDK, Google it* T-shirt. I'll probably wear my all-white Vans. I only need to decide if I'm going to wear hoops or stud earrings and bracelets or a watch."

"Whatever. Where is the charger?" he asks with his hand out.

"I need your help with picking a submission topic."

"Submission topic?"

"Hello! I told you guys about my school's online magazine the other day at dinner," I say. "No one ever listens to me."

Enrique rubs his chin and frowns. "Nope, I don't remember that. What's the big deal? Just write about braiding hair and all the other junk you like."

"No."

"Why not? It will be easy because it's something you like," he says, looking around my room.

"Why not?" I say, sitting down on my bed and staring at the wall. "Because I want my submission to stand out and be different from all the other girls' topics. And you know what? Maybe I'm overthinking it. It doesn't have to be the perfect topic. If I write a really good article, it won't matter what topic I write about. My skills are what will shine and get me picked for the magazine."

"Umm, okay, great," Enrique says. He spots my charger hanging out of the outlet near my bed and snatches it out. "You better hurry up and get dressed. Ma said we're leaving at 2:30."

We pull into Tía Fina's driveway, and I hear loud laughs coming from the backyard. I hop out of the car before it completely stops. I wanted out the moment Pa announced we would be stopping to pick up Abuela. She spent the whole ride here talking mess about her landscaper because he cut her rose bushes too low. I spent the entire ride biting my inner cheek so I wouldn't yell out, *Why is Abuela coming with us? This is Ma's side of the family, not hers.*

I take long strides up the driveway to the garage, where my cousins and all the "young people," as the adults call us, are hanging out texting, playing cards, talking, and listening to music.

Pa and Ma head into the house while Enrique daps up all the boys. I shoot Abuela a look that says, *Go with the adults.* Too bad she doesn't see it. Since this isn't the first time she has come to a party here. Abuela walks around the garage, telling all the boys how much they've grown since the last time she's seen them and asking all the older girls, "¿Y tu novio?" I have no idea why she cares if they have boyfriends.

"You look cute, girl," my cousin Ayesha says, hugging me. "I'm lovin' your braids."

"Thanks, boo." Ayesha has two older brothers, Albert and Paul; she's a little sister like me.

A few other cousins come by and gush over my braids. I look over at Abuela, and this time she *is* watching. I hope she realizes that she is the only person who hates braids. She curls up one side of her mouth and looks at my hair. If she says something mean, I'm going off. But she walks to the door and goes inside the house.

After chatting with everyone in the garage, I go through the house to the backyard, where the party is. Tía Fina is Ma's older sister and today is her birthday, so the yard is decorated in her favorite color: black. Tía always says, "Black is chic and makes you look skinny."

"Feliz cumpleaños, Tía!" I say when I spot her. "I like your skirt."

"Gracias," she says, spinning around in a circle.

Tía has been a fashionista way before the word ever existed. Ma says that's part of the reason why we call her "Fina," because she's always so refined and elegant. Tía has an eye for putting things together and making them work. Today is no different. She's wearing a shimmery sequined slim-fitting skirt, a form-fitting black tank top, and heels. Her accessories dangle and shine as she glides around, talking to everyone.

Tía Fina is the one who taught me the importance of accessories and how they "make your outfit." I was in second grade when she told me to never leave home without earrings and gave me my first pair of solid gold hoops.

Her backyard is full of people. I greet family with kisses on the cheek and get greeted with "Wa-Pin little (pronounced *likkle*) Carmen" from people I've never met before, people who tell me they remember when my mom was pregnant with me or remember when I was a baby.

I pass by Pa and a group of men drinking something brown in clear plastic cups, talking about life in Panamá and growing up in the Müeller building in Panamá City. A few tables are pushed together to the side of the patio and covered with a tablecloth. Tin pans of carimañolas, pig feet, arroz con pollo, ensalada de papa, and empanadas are spread out on the tables.

There are also a few trays of olives and cheese on frill-tipped toothpicks. A white birthday cake with strawberries sits in the middle of everything. At the far end of the table are the drinks: water, soda, Seco, and Evelyn's favorite, Sorrel.

I fill my plate with as much of everything as possible when Miriam Makeba's "Pata Pata" starts to play. For the adults, this song means it's time to dance. For me, it means it's time to go inside.

Michael Sado

You havin fun???

Sicily Jordan

Yeah. But this is more of an old people party, LOL.

I stay on Tía Fina's couch for about twenty minutes texting with Michael when Tía comes into the house from the backyard, holding empty tin pans that she puts on the counter.

"How come you're not outside?" she asks.

"I'm so full, and the garage is getting cooler," I lie. I really stayed inside to text Michael without Enrique or any of my cousins getting into my business.

She drops down next to me on the couch, leans her head back, and exhales loudly.

"My feet are killing me," she says. "So, what's up? What's new? I haven't talked to you all night. And it's been a while since we've had one of our phone calls where you catch me up on all the fancy stuff you have going on."

I giggle. I love it when Tía asks to hear about my "fancy" stuff. It makes me feel like I'm some important person who lives a glamorous life.

"Nothing much," I say. "Just trying to figure out what to write for my school's online magazine."

"Write about us, your family."

"Tía, no one wants to read about us," I laugh. "We're not interesting."

"Yes, we are. ¡Somos Panameños!" she says with her fist in the air. "Or you can write about braiding. That's something you like." She points at my braids. "And you did a good job."

"This?" I say, pointing at my hair too. "My friend did this. I'm still practicing, trying to get to her level."

"You still know how to do it, though. Maybe write a how-to guide. Teach people how to braid or write about the history of braids."

"I don't know about that. I mean, I don't think the kids at my school would be interested in reading that. The majority of them have a different kind of hair texture, if you know what I mean."

"Yup, I know what you mean," she confirms. "Still, our hair is worth being talked about and praised. Braids started in Africa and hair was braided in different styles as a way to tell which community or tribe you belonged to. In slavery days, here in the US, and in other countries too, Black women's natural hairstyles were seen as unkempt and even dirty."

"Really?" I say, suddenly wishing my journal was with me to write down what Tía is telling me.

"*Really*, and many slave owners' wives were jealous of how our hair could be done in so many different styles. Out of that jealously came a law that said enslaved women had to cover their natural hair. And even in present-day Panamá, a mother had to fight with her daughter's school just so her daughter could wear her hair in braids to class."

"Like recently?" I ask.

"Sadly, yes. But out of that mother's fight, a beautiful celebration was started in 2012. When you have a chance, look up Día de la Trenzas."

"What's that?"

"Day of the Braids. It's a celebration that happens in Panamá every third Monday in May, during Etnia Negra." I can't believe this. Abuela goes to Panamá all the time. There is no way she's never heard of this celebration. If the whole country is learning to accept braids and has a day dedicated to them, how can she still feel the way she does?

"Josefina, come and dance. Your song is on," a woman

shouts into the house from the sliding glass door. I haven't heard anyone use Tía's full name in a long time.

"Oh, I hear it! Here I come!" Tía gets up from the couch, does a limp shuffle walk to the door, and then turns back toward me.

"Keep practicing your braiding, Sicily. You'll get it. And remember, your hair is your crown. Hold it up high."

TWENTY-THREE

I Thought We Were BFFs

LUNCH IS THE only time of day when all of us students are in the same place at the same time. The loud voices and screams of laughter that come from students seated at rows and rows of gray lunch tables echo loudly under the metal patio cover that stands tall above us.

I'm with Kamaya, Kiara, and Reyna. My crew. My girls. My friends. Like every day for the last few weeks, today is no different as the four of us sit at *our* table during lunch listening to Kamaya catch us up on her newest "cutie of the day."

"He is everything, y'all. And he's on the track team. I saw him running laps around the field this morning before school started. He is so fine," Kamaya says. She puts both palms onto her chest and looks up to the sky. "He bleached the top of his hair, *uhh*, I love it. Yesterday he walked past me, and I swear I almost passed out."

Reyna and I look at each other and laugh.

"What's his name?" Kiara asks.

"I don't know. I don't even know him," Kamaya says as if we should have known that. The three of us crack up laughing with her.

Something about the way the warm sun hits my left cheek makes me sleepy. If we were allowed, I would go over to the grassy area near the library and nap.

While my friends chat about their favorite acrylic nail shapes, I put on Reyna's sunglasses and slide my bracelets off my wrist and rest my head down on my folded arms. I close my eyes and relax as the sun covers my cheek like a warm washcloth.

"Let me borrow a dollar to get a bag of chips."

My muscles stiffen, and my ears perk up. I know that voice.

"No! Don't you have your own money?" Reyna says.

"Come on. I forgot my wallet at home."

I lift my head and open my eyes to see Michael standing to the side of me, at the end of the lunch table.

I breathe in small amounts of air through my teeth and take off Reyna's sunglasses while smiling at him.

"Aye, wassup, Sis?" Michael says to me. "You know, short for Sicily—get it?"

Thump. Thump.

"Yeah, I get it." I take a deep breath to steady my heartbeat

204

and look Michael up and down, from head to toe. Something is different—a haircut. His familiar curly hair is gone. Michael's hair is now cut low on the top and shaved off on the sides.

"Fine. You better pay me back as soon as we get home," Reyna says, searching through her crossbody bag.

"Yeah, yeah. I'll pay you back," Michael says. He snatches four quarters from Reyna and walks away.

"*Sis*. I know you guys are cool, but nicknames?" Reyna says.

"Stop it." I roll my eyes. "That's the first time he's ever called me that."

"He looks cuter than the last time I saw him," Kamaya says.

With a deep side-eye, I watch her stare at Michael as he walks away.

"Yeah, I agree. He's definitely gets cuter every day," Kiara says, staring at Michael too.

I sit up straight, then inhale and exhale loudly. Both of them need to stop talking about and looking at *my* Michael. Go back to talking about all the other boys.

"How old is he again?" Kamaya asks. "And what grade is he in?"

"Yuck," Reyna says. "He's in seventh grade, and he's twelve or something. I can't remember." She rolls her eyes. "If you have any more questions, direct them to Sicily. Or, *oops*,

I mean *Sis*." Reyna points at me. "She probably knows more about him than I do."

"Relax," I say, as my left knee starts to bounce. "Why are you making such a big deal about him calling me that?"

"Yeah, who cares what Michael calls her?" Kamaya says. "Give us some real info. Does he have a girlfriend?"

Reyna leans in toward the middle of the table, and Kamaya and Kiara do the same. I stay still for a second, a little worried about what tea Reyna is about to spill about Michael. Is she going to tell us something embarrassing? Something funny? Or something she can't stand about him? I shoo away the instinct telling me to stay out of the conversation and lean in with them.

Reyna opens her mouth, then backs away from us.

"Come on. Spill it," Kiara says.

"I don't know if he has a girlfriend," Reyna whispers. She drops her head back and lets out the loudest laugh. A few people turn to look at her.

"Oh, you jerk! I thought you were gonna tell us something juicy," Kamaya says, sitting straight up. While Kamaya and Kiara look disappointed, I am relieved. I don't want to hear any more secrets Michael and Reyna have about each other.

"Let's talk about something else, please," Reyna says. "It's bad enough that he lives with me, and I see him all the time. I don't want to have to spend my lunch break being forced to talk about him too."

I'm scanning the wall outside of the lunchroom to see if the line is shorter when Michael comes out holding a can of soda and an orange bag of chips—Cheetos, probably. He's walking back toward the lunch tables when Erin Masterson comes out of nowhere. She puts her hand on his shoulder and stops him.

"Right, Sicily?" Kamaya asks me.

"Huh, what?" I say.

Reyna turns in the direction I'm looking.

"Staring at Michael?" she says, waving her finger at me. "I feel like you two have something going on."

"It's not even like that," I say. "I was distracted. I thought I saw Erin Masterson coming our way."

"*Sure*, or you were too busy daydreaming about my cousin." Reyna bumps Kiara's arm with her elbow, and they both start laughing. "*Sis*. Come on," Reyna says. "You guys text all the time, and you have secret meetings in the library after school."

"It was no secret," I say, shaking my head. "We were there for the online magazine. I even invited you to the first meeting, and you passed on going with me."

Ignoring my explanation, Reyna turns and says to Kiara, "I'm surprised she hasn't shown up to my house to hang out with him instead of me," as if I'm not sitting right across from her.

"What are you talking about?" I ask her with a back-off-of-me tone of voice. When she faces me, I look Reyna in her eyes and she stares right back into mine. I'm so confused. *What's her problem?*

"Chill, Sicily. She's just joking," Kamaya says.

"Well, not really," Reyna says. "I don't get why Sicily's acting like it's not true."

"Anyway, look at him," Kiara says, pointing at some boy sitting at another table. "He's cute."

I break eye contact with Reyna and look off into the distance. No one responds to Kiara's comment. The mood at the table has shifted, and goosebumps cover my arms. I suddenly feel like they've made me the punch line of their inside joke. Why is Reyna picking on me? What did I do to her? Instead of turning this into a big deal, I decide to take Kamaya's advice to chill.

"Have you guys seen the preview for the new Michael B. Jordan movie?" I ask. "Now, *he* is fine."

"That's right," Kamaya says.

"Yassss," Kiara adds.

"He definitely is," Reyna says. "Hey, *Sis*. I bet you think *your* Michael is cuter though. Right?"

And that, right there, does it. Anger boils inside me and mixes with all the feelings I still have about Abuela, my ruined pollera, the stress of my submission, and petty Erin Masterson.

I explode.

I slam my palms down onto the table and push myself up to my feet.

"Michael was right about you," I shout. "You latch on to things and just can't let them go. Like, it's one thing to make a joke. But at some point, you're supposed to stop!" Reyna's mouth drops open and forms a perfect *O*. I'm not sure who is more shocked: her or me. Only I've had enough, so I ignore the stares from everyone around us and keep going. "You just keep coming for me. I thought we were BFFs. Now I'm not so sure. My best friend isn't supposed to make me into a joke and embarrass me."

"I don't think she's trying to embarrass you, Sicily," Kiara says.

"Yeah. She just doesn't want you to keep secrets from her," Kamaya adds.

It's obvious Reyna has already told Kamaya and Kiara how she feels about all this. *Why didn't she talk to me?* Without saying anything else, I bend down, pick up my school bag, and walk away from the table. All the feelings I had at the beginning of lunch about them being my crew go in one direction as I walk away in another.

TWENTY-FOUR

Practice Makes Perfect

"OKAY, GIRL. I'M sitting on the floor in front of the mirror, and I have everything here: edge control, a rattail comb, and a few packs of hair," I say, lifting everything one by one so she can see them.

"Good. I'll talk you through this very slowly," Evelyn tells me.

"Wait, hold up," I tell her. I pick up my phone and push the top volume button a few times on the side. "Okay, now I'm ready," I say. I snap my phone into the suction thing attached to the mirror at eye level so that Evelyn can see my every move.

Since Saturday, Ma has been telling me to take out the braids Evelyn did because they are too tight and will pull my baby hairs out. I finally listened and unbraided my hair after school today, mostly as a way to take my mind off what happened with Reyna during lunch.

When Evelyn texted me this afternoon, I explained why I had to take the braids out, and she offered to give me instructions over FaceTime so I could re-create the same style but not as tight.

"I pretty much know how to cornrow. I need a lot of help adding in the hair extensions. I mean, I can do it. I just have to practice more so the braids aren't so sloppy."

"No worries, I got you."

Hearing Evelyn say that makes me feel good, and that old feeling of wishing I could go to Ravenwood comes back. Evelyn and the rest of the Tether Squad would never treat me the way Reyna did today. I think back to my old "Why I Hate My New School" list and mentally add another.

#7 Being betrayed by one of my BFFs

"Okay, so I have my sections, and the first hair extension is ready. What's next?" I ask.

"Slide your fingers over to the opposite side and grab the other section of hair. Remember, don't let go of the fake hair."

I start doing what Evelyn says. Her words go through my ears and slide up to my brain. But for some reason, they don't reach my hands. My fingers seem like they are lost and confused in my hair. It's like braiding is suddenly foreign to them.

"Steady your hands, girl," Evelyn shouts. "You look like you're nervous or something."

"Let me start over," I say. I pull out the fake hair extension and claw my fingers through, untangling it. I want to tell Evelyn all about what happened with Reyna today and explain that I'm not nervous, only annoyed. I just want to put it all behind me. Besides, I did nothing wrong. Reyna's the one who needs to apologize to me.

"There you go, keep your fingers relaxed. Now do that same thing again in the opposite direction," Evelyn says. "Turn your head to the side. Good. *Good*. See? You're getting it."

"Are you sure?" I ask her. "The braid looks a little puffy."

"You have to figure out how to braid tight enough for it not to be puffy, but not so tight that it breaks your real hair out. I'm still learning that," Evelyn admits. "And what you're doing looks fine. Practice makes perfect," she says.

"Yeah, yeah. You sound like my mom." We laugh.

"Keep going. Under the middle section, reach and grab, and add more hair in there. Good, now do it again," Evelyn instructs.

I listen to her words, and finally, my fingers find their rhythm. They confidently finish the cornrow, and I braid the rest of the hair extension all the way down to the end of the hair. I turn my back to my phone so Evelyn can see the braid.

"Ugh. This is the one thing I hate about braiding. The hair gets all over the place," I say. Somehow strands have wrapped themselves around my ankles and feet. I wiggle my toes to free them, but that only makes it worse.

"It's looking good, Sicily. I'm telling you, keep practicing. You will get it. When my sister taught me, I practiced every day on one of my dolls. A month later, I had it."

"A doll? That's a good idea," I say. "Okay, I'm gonna try this next braid by myself. You just watch."

As I grab some more fake hair from the pack, Abuela walks past my open bedroom door. I pretend not to see her and position my fingers in my hair.

"Here I go," I say to Evelyn. I repeat the same steps she gave me with the first braid. I go slowly, weaving my fingers through my hair as it creates a braid pattern that I am instantly proud of.

"Hi," Evelyn says. I look from the mirror to my phone and see Evelyn waving. I look back to the mirror and see her standing behind me, waving back to my phone. Abuela.

"I'm gonna keep going," I tell Evelyn, "and I'll talk to you later."

"Okay. Send me a pic when you finish," Evenly says, and we end our FaceTime.

"Hola, mi amor," Abuela says, sitting down on my bed. She is wearing a red shirt that says, *Someone in Panamá Loves Me*. I shake my head and roll my eyes.

"Hi," I respond in an all-business tone of voice. Then I remember how I barely missed getting grounded for being mean to Abuela last week and check myself real quick. I go back to braiding my hair and try to ignore her. But my closet door mirrors reflect my whole bedroom, and there is no way I can't *not* see her. As much as I try not to, I keep making eye contact with Abuela.

Is she going to say something?

Actually, I'd rather she not say anything. I don't want to hear it. I continue braiding and whispering Evelyn's directions to myself, and again, my fingers are stiff and confused. I try braiding the same hair over and over again, and I can't relax enough to get the hair to slide into the right place. I should call Evelyn back. Listening to her helped me focus and take my mind off Reyna. Now I need her directions to help me take my mind off Abuela.

"Ugh." I slam my hand down to the floor in front of me. "I can't do this."

Abuela sitting there, silently watching, is making me super nervous. Why is she here? What is she about to say? She hates my braids, so why is she watching me try to do this? She's probably waiting for the perfect time to repeat what she said to me last time. Or maybe she's thought of something worse to say.

I take a deep breath and raise my hands to my head and start my braid over again. In the mirror, I see Abuela wincing and rubbing her fingers. Her small eyes are tightly shut, and her teeth are pressed together like the pain is suddenly too much.

"Why aren't you wearing your gloves?" I ask without thinking.

I miss her. First I lost Abuelo, and now I've lost Abuela too—just in a different way. I wish I could talk to her about everything I'm going through right now. I even want to share all the different feelings I have for Michael.

Her eyes open slowly. "I don't like them," she says. "They help with the swelling, but they make holding stuff even harder for me."

"Oh."

"Everyone on Saturday loved your braids so much," Abuela says.

"Yeah, *Ma's* family *always* has nice things to say to me." I look at her reflection in the mirror, and she shifts her eyes away from mine. And I shift my eyes too, making sure I don't break eye contact.

"That's good," she says.

"Everywhere else I go . . ." I pause and shake my head from side to side. ". . . people love to tell me how ugly my braids are. Here at home and even at school." Abuela sits up straight and starts pulling her shirt collar back and forth, allowing air to cool her neck and face.

Good.

I'm glad she is catching these jabs I'm throwing at her. "You know what? I don't care what people think." I shrug my shoulders, tilt my head, and wait for a response.

Abuela wrinkles her forehead and stands. I can't tell if she is mad or not. Oh well, I'm over letting what she said about my hair bother me. Like Reyna, Abuela also needs to apologize if she wants us to be cool again.

TWENTY-FIVE

I'm Over It

THERE SHE IS. Just do it, Sicily.

"Reyna," I say in a low voice from a distance as we enter campus. Other people are walking and filling in the gap between us, so I know there is no way she hears me calling her. I low-key don't want her to hear me. If she doesn't hear me, then she won't turn around. And if she doesn't turn around, I won't have to talk to her. And if I don't have to talk to her, I can go on acting like I tried and continue feeling like it's only Reyna who needs to apologize.

Last night, after I gave up on braiding my hair, I slicked it back into a low ponytail and put on my headscarf. I crawled into bed way before it was time for me to go to sleep and thought that maybe, just maybe, I did too much yesterday. I mean, I knew Reyna was joking around with me. I probably shouldn't have yelled at her.

The last time Enrique and I got into a fight, I acted the same way. When Ma got home and caught me screaming at him at the top of my lungs, she separated us and asked me how I could have handled things differently. I've been asking myself that same question about yesterday.

With three minutes until the morning bell rings, the courtyard is bursting with students. Ma usually drops me off way earlier than this, but she was running late this morning— which ruined my plan to talk to Reyna before class.

I turn and head to the 200s and catch another glimpse of Reyna through the crowd. There are so many people blocking my view of her that I stop walking and stand on my tippy-toes so I can see over the tops of people's heads. At the bench where *we* always meet in the morning, I see Reyna sitting there talking to Kiara. Reyna is wearing a beautiful bright yellow, pink, and green flower crown that perfectly matches the sandals she has on.

I drop my head down. Kamaya was right. I shouldn't have kept a secret from my best friend. I should have told Reyna how I feel about her cousin. I just didn't want her being mad at me for liking him, and it happened anyway.

Do it. Say sorry.

As I get closer to the bench where Reyna, Kiara, and now Kamaya are, my hands start to shake. My neck is a little moist, so I wrap my coily curls into a bun so I can cool down. What if I try to talk to Reyna and she yells at me? Or walks away from me? And what about Kiara and Kamaya? Whose side are they on? Probably Reyna's. I mean, she is the one who introduced me to them. They were her friends, not mine. Reyna and I are like two parents who've divorced, and Kiara and Kamaya are like the kids who don't have a choice about who they go with. Except these two *do* have a choice, and I can see that it's Reyna.

Stop being scared.

I walk a little closer to the bench, and then the bell rings. People walk in front of me and around me, bump into me, and even trip over me.

I don't move. I have to do this now. I bend my knees and ball up my fists. When I straighten my legs, I shout with everything inside me, "Reyna! Reyna!" I'm so loud that a bunch of people (not named Reyna) turn and stare at me. Reyna hears me too. She turns around and looks directly at me. I let out a long breath and start moving in her direction.

I stop when she lowers her eyelids, spins back around, and keeps walking to class. I didn't really think she would react this way. I thought Reyna would come talk to me so we could work things out. I stare down at my feet as people walk past me before finally heading to my classroom. I guess that's it. Just as fast as Reyna and I became friends again, I ruined our friendship.

At my desk, I sit with my shoulders back and my head and eyes pointing straight ahead. I try my hardest not to look even slightly in Reyna's direction. I want to pass her a note. I want to giggle with her about Mrs. Taylor's clunky clog shoes, and I want to ask her if I can borrow the metallic nail polish she's wearing. Most important, I want to ask her if she will forgive me for yelling at her.

The way Reyna looked at me when I called her name in the courtyard makes me think I should just leave her alone. So I turn my head and stare out the window while Mrs. Taylor reads to the class from a book called *Wonder*. It's about a boy named Auggie Pullman who was born with a facial deformity. Hearing Mrs. Taylor read about how Auggie deals with constant stares and mean reactions to his face makes me feel even sadder.

The rest of the day flies by in a miserable mess. I start to think that maybe I should try harder with Reyna.

I ditch that plan when Mrs. Taylor makes a joke. Out of habit, Reyna and I turn toward each other and laugh. Two seconds into the laugh, Reyna stops and turns away from me. I slide down in my cold hard chair and put my head down. I've officially lost my friend.

When the end-of-school bell rings, I rush out of my desk and push the classroom door open so hard that it catches wind, slams against the rail, and makes the ramp vibrate. I fly out of the classroom for two reasons: One, I don't want Mrs. Taylor to say anything to me about swinging the door open so hard. And two, I don't want to see Reyna any longer than I have to.

"Aye, Sicily." A palm grips my shoulder. As I turn my head, I see the white wristband, which confirms what I already knew. It's Michael.

"I texted you three times last night. Wassup?" he asks. We move over to the side, out of people's way as they rush to leave school.

"Um. I, um. Really? I don't think I got them." I search his face for any hints that he might be mad at me. The only thing I notice is a smirk that says, *You're lying*. And he's right. I saw all three of his text messages at the exact moments they each showed up on my phone. I didn't respond because by the time he sent the first one, I had already imagined Reyna yelled at him for talking mess about her to me. Since all three of his messages only said, "Hey," I figured Michael was just reaching out to tell me he was mad at me for repeating what he told me. Or maybe Reyna didn't say anything to him about it, and I just need to relax.

"So, um. Yeah, about pictures for my submission. I was—"

"Why did you tell Reyna what I said about her?"

Shoot. "Sorry" flies out of my mouth almost faster than I can open it. If I can fix this problem right away, I won't have to worry about *two* of my friends hating me.

221

"It's cool. It makes things at home a little messy. But I don't care. It wasn't like I was lying."

"Oh, thank God," I say, wrapping my arms around his neck and pulling him close to me. "Um, oops, sorry." I take a step back from him and bite my bottom lip.

"No problem. I gotta go. B-ball practice at the park." Michael starts walking backward while staring at me, just like he did the day he knocked me down on Reyna's front porch. "I'll text you later."

I slam my bedroom door shut and lie on my bed like a starfish, with my arms and legs hanging off the edges. My phone vibrates in my back pocket. I snatch it out, hoping it's Reyna responding to the text I sent her while walking home after school today.

Evelyn Martin
Sicily! Im dying to see how your braids turned out. SEND PICS!!

Samara Smith
Who braided Sicilys hair?

Evelyn Martin
I taught her on FaceTime.

Samara Smith
Teach me!

Me too. I wanna learn.

Show us Sicily!

I got caught up with something else and didnt get to finish 😔

The Tether Squad then plans a day for us to go to Evelyn's so she can teach us all how to braid. I tap out of the group chat and tap on a notification that leads me to unanswered DMs and a list of new followers that includes the *Chisholm Is Talking* page.

The page doesn't have much of anything, just the words *We Are Chisholm* as the profile picture and one post that says, *Coming Soon* in bright orange and blue letters. Under the picture is one comment from Erin Masterson: "Shirley Chisholm Middle School is pleased to announce that we will soon be launching *Chisholm Is Talking*, an online magazine. This year's eighth graders created the magazine, and all articles will be written only by eighth graders. Stay tuned. It's going to be good!!!!"

Is she serious? EIGHTH GRADERS WILL WRITE ALL ARTICLES?

Isn't Mr. Marconi overseeing this page? Why would he let her post that?

Chill, Sicily.

They wouldn't have opened the magazine meeting up to all students if it were only for eighth graders.

I tap on Erin Masterson's page and immediately roll my eyes. I scroll down a little and see that all the pictures she has posted within the last two weeks are selfies with her lips poking out.

Who still does duck lips in their selfies?

I keep scrolling and scrolling down with my pointer finger. Of course, more selfies. And then there are pictures of her posing with expensive handbags. There are also some pictures of her kissing her passport. Does she think she's the only one who has one of those? I've had mine since I was two, for my first trip to Panamá.

There are a few rows of pictures taken at a beach house. One of them shows her with people I assume are her parents. She looks just like her dad. The two hold up two fingers, making the peace sign, while her mother smizes and pouts her lips. Erin Masterson's dad is tagged, so I click and scroll through his page just to be nosy.

He has pictures of himself shaking hands with different people. He's wearing a yellow construction hat in every post and a blue or black suit. I'm about to go back to my page when I recognize someone in one of the photos. It's Principal Rivas. Erin Masterson's dad and my school principal are holding shovels and digging in the dirt. The caption says, "Chisholm's

Groundbreaking Ceremony." I keep scrolling and see pictures with a lot of teachers I've seen around school. Even Mr. Marconi is in one of them. Erin Masterson's dad and Mr. Marconi are smiling like they are old friends.

Maybe she wasn't lying when she said her dad and Mr. Marconi agreed on no sixth graders writing for the magazine.

A DM notification from Erin Masterson pops up on my screen:

ErinMTheBest

> Why did you like my pic???? GET OFF MY PAGE!!!!

What is she talking about? I close the DM, go back to her page, and quickly scan through the selfie pictures. And there it is, a red heart under a picture of her making a kissy-face and holding a Starbucks cup. *Shoot!* What do I do? Unlike it? She already knows I'm snooping on her page.

ErinMTheBest

> Don't waste your time writing a submission. You're not getting picked. I've made sure of it.

My fingers are itching to tap letters and form words. What do I say? I'm no longer sure that she was lying about how much control she has over the magazine and who gets picked. I mean, her dad knows *everybody*.

Why only eighth-grade writers? Why is that so important to her? I wonder if she's going this hard on the other sixth and seventh graders who were at the magazine meetings or if it's just me. What did I ever do to her?

I put my phone down on the bed next to me and stare at the floor. I wish I could call Reyna for help. She always knows what to say in the moment, while I never have a comeback until hours later.

ErinMTheBest

Anything you planned on writing about wouldn't get picked anyway. You're a little kid who knows nothing about writing.

Ugh. I'm sick of everyone and everything. Why did I ever think writing again was a good idea? Maybe Ma was right. Writing shouldn't be this important. Look at all this drama I'm going through. It should just be a hobby like she said.

I get up from my bed, stomp over to my desk, and snatch my glitter spiral notebook. Why did I think I could do this without Abuelo? I flip through to the page that has my magazine submission ideas and tear it out. I rip the page over and over into tiny little pieces and let them rain down to the floor. I'm tired of hearing the same thing over and over from Erin

Masterson, and I'm tired of everyone treating my gut like it's a punching bag.

I'm done with the school magazine, Erin Masterson, Reyna—well, not really Reyna—but Abuela, for sure. I'm over it all.

TWENTY-SIX

Afro

"**PLEASE LET HER** have written back." After dinner, I run upstairs to my room, where I purposely left my phone after texting Reyna twice asking her if we could talk. On my bed, my phone is lit up with a notification. But it's a news alert about a fire in the mountains.

I open the text chat and write her again. *Please.*

I stare at the text box, wishing for those three little bubbles to appear letting me know Reyna's writing back. Sadly, I get nothing. Maybe she's busy and hasn't seen any of my messages yet. I'll give her some time to write back, and by tonight, I'm sure we'll be all good.

After what happened earlier with Erin Masterson online, I decide to stay off that app for the rest of the night. I had planned to use this time to work on my magazine submission. But my ideas are now at the bottom of the plastic trash can next to my desk. I finished my homework before dinner, and there's nothing good on TV until eight, and I think I've watched everything on my Netflix list.

There is nothing else for me to do so I pull up the *Teen Vogue* website and get lost clicking through some articles. I've almost finished reading a profile on Zendaya when Ma sticks her head in my room.

"Sicily, I'm going to Target. Meet me downstairs in five minutes," she says, then disappears.

"I'm just gonna stay home, Ma," I shout. Her footsteps stop in the hallway, then get louder as she comes back to my room.

"You always want to go to Target." Ma rushes over and puts the back of her hand up to my forehead. "Are you okay?" she asks.

"Yeah, fine." I get up and give Ma space to sit.

"These last few weeks, something has been off with you. Even during dinner earlier, you looked mad and annoyed with the world. Pa is starting to get very concerned. You know he's not okay when you and Enrique are upset."

Ma tilts her head to the side and squints her eyes at me. This is the face she makes when she knows I'm not being honest with her. It's way nicer than her *I know you're lying to me* face. In Ma's book, not being honest and lying are two different things. Not being honest with her is mostly about hiding how I feel. Lying to her means I'm hiding something I did because I know I'll get in trouble.

I stare back at Ma in silence. I'm not telling her about what happened with Reyna. And I'm definitely not telling her about everything that has been going on with Erin Masterson. I don't want her and Pa thinking there is a problem that needs to be solved by talking to my principal. Unlike Erin Masterson, I don't like having my parents involved in everything at school. Besides, I'm not submitting anything for the online magazine, so the Erin Masterson problem is solved. So what is it that Ma thinks I'm not being honest about?

Shoot. Did she find my pollera? No. She couldn't have. I've been doing an excellent job of keeping the closet doors closed. And every day since the spill, I have checked my laundry basket to make sure the pollera is still snug at the bottom.

But I stopped checking a few days ago to avoid the awful dirty-clothes smell oozing from the basket. I've been trying to wash my clothes in small piles to get rid of the stench. It's been hard because I have to make sure I only wash a few things at a time so my laundry basket stays full enough to hide the pollera.

Someone must have told Ma about it. Was it Mrs. Taylor following up to see if the stain came out? Reyna, as a way to get back at me? Or maybe this is a sign from God? Ma always says God will send us signs letting us know when we need to do something. Does He want me to come clean right now? I rub my sweaty hands together.

Maybe I should. I mean, I have no plan for cleaning it, and it can't sit in my closet forever. I need to get this over with and stop dragging it out. The longer this goes on, the worse my punishment will be.

I take a deep breath and exhale slowly.

"Ma . . ." I start. "Um . . ." And then something happens. Ma starts tapping her foot on the floor, making my bed sway. If I didn't know any better, I would have thought we were having a small earthquake. This is Ma's *I have something to talk to you about* foot tap. Could this be a *different* sign telling me I don't have to come clean? Ma is the one who has some-thing *she* wants to talk about. Thanks, God.

"What's going on, Ma?" I ask.

"Sicily, why isn't your hair braided?"

"What?" I place my hand on top of my head and move it down to my low ponytail. "Why?"

"I've been thinking about this all day since seeing you this morning. Did you stop braiding your hair because of what your abuela said to you?"

"No, Ma. I was struggling yesterday. So I gave up. I'm gonna try again this weekend."

Ma lets out a long breath of air that she was probably holding since she walked into my room.

"Good." She smiles. "Do you want me to do something to last you till the weekend?"

"Okay." I lie down on the floor and pull a pack of hair

231

extensions from under my bed and sit in between Ma's legs. I slide the elastic hair tie out of my ponytail and rest my arms on her knees. Ma is a pro. She uses her fingernails like a comb to separate my hair. She divides the right amount of hair extensions from the pack and starts braiding.

"I did think about it though." I start moving my arms, causing Ma's legs to swing in and out. She hates it when I do this but doesn't stop me this time.

"What do you mean?"

"I thought about not braiding my hair anymore so that Abuela wouldn't say anything else to me." I close my eyes and continue talking. "Sometimes, out of nowhere, I'll hear her voice in my head saying I look ghetto and low-class—that braids are for girls with pelo malo. I don't see Abuela the way I used to anymore. She's a stranger to me." I pause and open my eyes. "Ma, why did she say those things to me?"

"Sicily, she loves you very much," Ma says, ignoring what I asked her.

"Hmph, doesn't seem like it," I say under my breath.

"Your Abuela has an old-school way of seeing things. She thinks relaxed hair is better than natural hair. There are a lot of things she and I don't see eye to eye on, and that is one of them."

"How come you never relaxed my hair?" I ask.

"Because I like your hair the way it is. When you were little, you used to fight me whenever I tried to comb it. Pa would have to hold you down while I would try to put some bows in your hair." She laughs. "You got a little better when you were about four. But by then, your hair was so thick and became such a pain to comb every morning that I started braiding it. My mom never relaxed my hair when I was growing up. I chose to do it when I moved here to the States. I want you to choose if you want to relax your hair or not when you're older."

"I don't think I'll ever relax my hair. I heard it feels like your head is on fire and stinks really bad."

"Yeah, you heard right. Sicily, if what Abuela said is still bothering you, don't hold it in. Talk to her. Tell her how you feel." Ma finishes braiding my hair into a cute French braid down the middle of my head, leading into a thick braid down my back.

"Wait. You and Pa wouldn't be mad if I did that?"

"No. We want you to stand up for yourself. Just don't be rude and disrespectful while talking to her. You can be honest with her."

I start moving my hand in a circular motion on the carpet, rounding up the leftover hair extension strands into a pile.

"How is school going?" Ma asks. "No one in your class is being mean to you, right?"

"What? Why would they?"

"Well, you told us how the kids in your class treated you

during your presentation. How are they treating you now?

"Fine. I think they've forgotten all about that by now."

"Good," Ma says.

"You know what? I've learned a lot since that happened."

"Like what?

"I've learned a lot about Panamá's history of slavery and more information about the people who built the canal. And the other day, I was scrolling online and found a page about people like us."

"People like us? What do you mean?"

"Afro-Latinx," I say. "That's what we are, right?"

"By definition, yes. We are from Latin America, and we have African ancestry." Ma sounds exactly like the post I read online.

"How come I've never heard you use that word before?" I ask.

"Afro-Latinx isn't a term I'm used to using. Here in the US, when people ask me about my background, I tell them I'm Panamanian. And when I was growing up in Panamá, people automatically assumed, because I am Black, that my family was descended from slaves, Afro-colonial, or from the West Indies."

"Right, to work on the canal," I say.

"Exactly. They are called Afro-Antillanos. You know, there are other terms you can use to describe yourself. Not just Afro-Latinx."

"Like what?" I ask.

"Afro-descendent, Afro-Panamanian . . . and there's Black Panamanian, negra, which means Black, and—"

"Wait!" I say, cutting her off. "I need to write all this in my journal."

"Why?

"I recently started researching and writing info about Panamá and our culture in here. So I don't forget anything," I explain, grabbing my journal from my desk.

"That's an excellent idea," Ma says.

I have her repeat all the terms for me slowly as I write them down.

"If asked about my background, can I just say I'm Panamanian? Like you do?"

"Of course. You can also say it in Spanish, *Panameña*," Ma says. "Another important thing you should write down is that *Afro* at the beginning of those words shows that we acknowledge our African roots. We are Black first, before anything else."

TWENTY-SEVEN

I Miss My Friend

IT'S BEEN TWO days. Two days of having to sit next to Reyna in class and pretend like we were never friends. Two days of eating at a different lunch table. Two days of feeling horrible for what I said to her. Two days without my best friend.

I close the car door and wave bye to Pa. Standing in this exact spot in front of Reyna's house reminds me of the last time he dropped me off here. On that day, I would have never imagined that my friendship with Reyna would be where it is today. I slowly walk up the driveway to her front door.

I rub my palms together like they are cold, then press Reyna's doorbell. After pressing it a second time, Reyna opens the door slightly, just enough to show half of her face. From what I can see of her, she doesn't look as mad as I thought she would.

236

"Can we, um, talk?" I ask, biting my bottom lip.

Reyna swings the door all the way open and stands there staring at me with a bag of Flamin' Hot Cheetos in her hand. Without saying a word, she comes outside, closes the door behind her, and walks past me.

Where is she going?

I turn and watch her walk away from me and her front door. Unsure if she wants to talk to me or not, I follow her without saying a word.

Reyna turns the corner and sits with her back straight up against her garage door. Again, I follow her lead and sit down next to her. I quietly stare down at my knees poking out of the holes in my jeans.

I look over at Reyna a few times. All she does is stare straight ahead at the house across the street while munching on hot Cheetos.

I clear my throat. "So . . . how have you been?" I shift my eyes toward Reyna. She's as still as a statue. No longer chewing, not moving, not opening her mouth to answer me. I fold my arms across my chest.

I shouldn't have come here. She didn't respond to my DMs or texts or answer any of my phone calls. At school she acts like I don't exist. Why did I think she would be okay with me just showing up at her house?

"Whatever," I whisper to myself. I get up from where we

are sitting and dust the back of my jeans off. If she's not going to talk to me, I'm not going to waste my time. I'll call Pa to come pick me up once I get to the end of her street.

I stomp down her driveway as tears start collecting in my eyes. No. I am not going to cry. I'm the one who has been trying to make things right. If Reyna's done with me, then I'm done with her too. When I get to the end of the driveway, I remember why I came over here. I miss my friend. I need to fix this now.

I drop my arms and turn back to Reyna.

"I shouldn't have freaked out on you," I blurt out. "You were being funny at first. Then out of nowhere, it was like I became the joke, and I didn't get why you would do that to me. It's just— Ugh, these last few weeks. Everyone has been coming for me nonstop: my abuela, Erin Masterson, our class. And I— I don't know." I stop rambling and take in some air. "I guess I didn't realize how all of that stuff was messing with me, and I took it all out on you. I'm sorry. I shouldn't have acted like that."

"Sicily, it's okay." Reyna waves her hand back and forth, motioning for me to come back. "We're good," she says.

"What? Really?" I ask. "Are you sure?"

"Yes," she says, finally looking at me. "I was totally joking with you about Michael. Well, kind of. You know, I saw you guys together in the library the other day, and then it dawned on me. Michael is the name Evelyn couldn't remember at your sleepover. And I've heard him talk about you to my sister a few times."

I bounce up on the balls of my feet a few times and try to hide my smile.

"You know, I was so scared to move back here," Reyna says, as she lowers her head down a little.

I stop bouncing and plant my feet flat on the ground. "Really, why?" I ask, tilting my head to the side.

"I didn't think I'd have any friends. Me and you didn't stay in touch, and I don't really remember anyone else from kindergarten, so I thought I'd be all by myself. Things were cool when I met Kamaya and Kiara. But they're each other's best friends, not mine."

I stare down at Reyna and listen as she talks, remembering that I sounded the same way when I found out I had to go to Chisholm.

"And then this thing with you and Michael. You never even told me that you and him were texting. A small part of me . . ." Reyna pauses and looks down at the ground. "Well, actually, a big part of me was scared you'd replace me with him."

"And a big part of me was scared that if you found out that I liked him, you'd dead our friendship. You know, because you hate him so much," I say, sliding my hands into my pockets.

"It's not that I hate him," Reyna says, looking away from

me. "Sometimes I want things to go back to how they were before he moved in. It's weird having a boy in the house. And it's even weirder to see my parents treat him like a king. It's always *Let's do this for Michael*, or *Make sure Michael likes it*, and *Wait, let Michael pick first*," Reyna says in a voice that I assume is supposed to be her mom's. "I know my parents want to make sure he's happy since his family isn't here." She looks down at her palm and starts picking at it. "Sometimes I want it to be just us: me, my mom and dad, and my sister."

"Wow," I say staring down at Reyna. "I didn't know all that was going on."

"Yeah. It's a lot. I'm sorry," she says. "For everything. What happened at lunch, ignoring your call and texts, and for lying."

"What? What did you lie about?"

"Your sleepover," she says, with her eyes looking everywhere else except me. "You might have been asleep when I told Evelyn I've had a boyfriend before. And, well, that isn't true."

"Why did you lie about that?"

"I was all up in what Evelyn was saying about liking boys and having boyfriends. I wanted to impress you and your friend and make it seem like I could relate to what she was talking about. But I've never had a boyfriend. I have had crushes on a few boys, nothing for real. It was a dumb thing to lie about."

I don't know what to say to this. Reyna always seems so

sure of herself. Like, she doesn't care what people think or say about her. She never seems to always be in her head or feelings like me.

"I really am sorry, Sicily. I can't believe I was being so petty with you."

"Yes, you were definitely being petty, but I wasn't being a good bestie either." I sit down next to her again, and she tilts her Cheetos bag toward me. Even though I hate hot Cheetos, I fish one out of the bag and suck on it until it's mild enough for me to chew and swallow.

"So you like Michael," Reyna says. This time when Reyna sorta, kinda asks, she only sounds curious.

"No. We're just friends. That's it."

"You *literally* just said you were scared about me finding out you like him," Reyna says, elbowing me and laughing.

"Okay, okay," I say. "I go back and forth about it. Some days I like him a lot. Then others, I'm all nervous and confused about him. It's so weird."

"Yeah, I know. But you definitely think he's pogi."

"Po—what?"

"Pogi. It's what Filipinos say when we think a guy is cute, handsome, bae."

"Um. I guess. Okay. Yes, he is pogi. You better not tell him I said that," I say, poking Reyna's arm with my finger.

"I won't say a thing." Reyna zips her lips with her two fingers and tosses away the fake key. "I promise."

"I really don't get why girls like Michael though. He is so gross," Reyna says.

"Yeah, I know it's weird. I still can't believe girls like my brother."

"You know, sometimes my dad has to force Michael into the bathroom to take a shower." She puts her hand on her stomach and puffs out her cheeks like her mouth has suddenly filled with something she must spit out immediately. "That boy is nasty," she adds.

"You can't keep doing that, Reyna," I say.

"What?" Reyna says playfully, with her shoulders and palms raised up near her ears.

"Keep talking mess about Michael. I get it, you don't like each other. I just don't want to be caught in the middle of you guys ever again."

"Okay. I'll stop talking about my dumb cousin in front of you."

I turn to face Reyna and widen my eyes.

"Ha! That was the last time. I promise," she says.

"So anyways," I say, hoping to move our conversation on to something else. "Please tell me you've seen those clog shoe things Mrs. Taylor has been wearing."

"OMG, yes. What are those?" Reyna says. "They make this weird clomping noise when she walks."

We crack up laughing and it feels good to have my friend back.

"Text me later, okay?" Reyna crumples up the Cheetos bag and stands.

"Why? What's wrong?" I ask.

Reyna motions with her head for me to look over to the side. I turn and see Michael walking toward us with a camera in his hand. And now I don't know what to do with myself. Even though I get all hot and nervous, I really like being around him.

"You guys better not talk about me again either," Reyna says, laughing.

"I learned my lesson," I tell her as she walks away. "I promise."

As Michael sits down where Reyna had been, he starts our conversation with a "wassup," like he always does.

"Hey," I say, turning my face away from him a little in case I have Cheeto breath.

"You and Reyna good now?"

"Yup. All good."

Michael starts clicking something on his camera as we sit for what seems like a long time in awkward silence. I want to tell him that I think he is so cute. And that I love his curly hair. And that I also love his hair when it's cut low. I want to tell him how excited I get when his name pops up on my phone and how happy I am that we're friends. And how much I like him as maybe more than a friend. Well, I will probably never tell him that last part. Instead of saying any of it out loud, I bend my knees and pull them close to my chest and hug my legs.

As I rest my chin on my knees, Michael finally breaks our silence. "So are you ready to send in your submission? It's due soon, right?"

"I'm not submitting anything."

"Why? What happened?"

"I'm just tired of dealing with Erin Masterson," I say, thinking about my "fight" with her yesterday.

"Erin *Masterson*. Ha! I think it's funny that you always say her last name."

I laugh with him. "I don't know why. For some reason, I feel like I always have to include it. She's so annoying though. I'll try out for the magazine again next year, when *Erin*, no last name, goes off to high school."

"She is *very* annoying, always hanging on me. One of her friends likes my boy Kevin. So they always come around giggling and stuff."

"Ha ha," I tease him.

"Yeah, ha ha." Michael turns his body and faces me. I look at him, then quickly look away. "Don't let her stop you," he says. "Remember, you said you wanted do it for your grandpa. He's going to love seeing your article in the school magazine."

I put my head down and smile. It's nice to know Michael remembers what I said that first time we messaged each other, but I still don't correct him about Abuelo.

Our conversation stops, and we sit in silence again while the sun starts to go down. The sky is now different shades of pink, red, and orange.

"This is kind of cool." Michael positions himself in different ways on the driveway, taking pictures of the sky from different angles.

"Yeah, this is kind of cool," I say, knowing that he's talking about the sky while I'm talking about us.

TWENTY-EIGHT

I'm Gonna Do It

I PLUG MY phone into the charger and change into my over-sized gray sweatpants and a T-shirt. Since leaving Reyna's house, I've thought a lot about what Michael said, and he's right. I can't let Erin Masterson stop me. Now I'm back at the starting line, trying to come up with a topic to write about again.

My list of ideas is ripped to pieces and gone. Even though I still remember most of them, I never thought they were all that interesting. I was just so desperate for a topic that I would have written about anything. That was then. Now that I'm for sure going to submit something, I have to write about what matters to me.

At my desk, I open my laptop. The stack of Abuelo's journals stares at me from the corner where my desk meets the wall. Since I can't read them and don't know where to put them, they've sat in that exact spot since I brought them up from Pa's office. Abuelo's blue journal, the twin to my pink one, is at the top of the stack. Looking at it reminds me that I need to write a fact in *my* journal for today.

On my computer, *Teen Vogue* is still on the screen from yesterday. On the site, I open the culture tab and see a profile about a London-based DJ. In the article, the DJ talks about her Afro–Puerto Rican background and shares her latest playlist. The list has over twenty songs that range from hip-hop, R & B, reggae, salsa, merengue, and Afrobeats. I will definitely be adding her playlist to my phone.

For me, it's the DJ herself, not the songs in her playlist, that gets my attention. In the article, there is a photo of her standing in a DJ booth. Ebony's her name and also a perfect way of describing her beautiful Black skin. Her long curly, kinky hair is everything, and I love the way the word "negra" shines against her skin on her necklace. Ebony's style is fly and speaks to who she is, a Black Latina, like me.

I open a new tab and look for popular music in Panamá to write about in my journal.

Dear Journal,

Today's fact is about reggaetón. Since Enrique felt that I should have talked about it in my class presentation, I decided to read about it. And that led to me learning about a different genre; well, actually, a movement that started in Panama way before reggaetón did.

In the early eighties, Renato performed as a hype man in dance halls in an area of Panama City called Río Abajo. He was the first person to translate and record English Jamaican reggae songs into Spanish. After he recorded and sold the songs to Diablos Rojos bus drivers, the music spread and became very popular. But non-Black Panamanians called it "Black people music."

This made me think about something I saw online a few days ago about erasure. At the time, I wasn't exactly sure what it meant. But after reading about how this discrimination as well as previous attempts by the Panamanian government to deny West Indians citizenship and kick them out of the country, I am now very clear on what it is. I also understand that one way to fight against erasure is through art like Renato did. He went on to write his own songs and he rapped about the discrimination Black Panamanians were experiencing at the time. This "Resistance Music Movement" was a way of uplifting Black people and fighting discrimination.

His first song, "El Deni," is a diss track to all the

Panamanian police officers who targeted young Black men and the culture. And Renato's second song, "La Chica de Los Ojos Café," celebrates Black women. These two songs are the first Spanish reggae songs ever recorded and were both huge hits in Panama.

Renato is the father of el Movimiento Urbano. He and other Panamanian reggae en Español artists not only translated the music into Spanish but also innovated the sound by creating dancehall riddims and fusions of their own.

Without reggae en Español, dancehall, hip-hop, and other musical genres, there would be no reggaetón, which means that without Renato's contribution to music, reggaetón would not be what it is today.

Sincerely.
Sicily

Abuelo always bounced his head up and down to the edited versions of hip-hop songs Enrique and I played around the house. Sometimes he even did a little shoulder bounce too. I'd bet all the money in my savings account, the one that I'm not allowed to touch until I turn twenty-one, that Abuelo was a fan of Renato and reggaetón music.

I look at his journals and grab the blue one. The faint

smell of the pain medication creme Abuelo used to rub on his shoulders fills my nose when I open it. Flipping from page to page, I squint my eyes at all the Spanish words, like that's somehow going to help my mind translate them to English.

Translate.

That's exactly what I'll do. On my computer, I go to a website that translates from one language to another. Just as I am about to type in what I assume is a title, since it's written at the top of one of the pages, I stop myself.

In Spanish it says, "Belen, mi amor." I don't need to translate this; I know that it says, "Belen, my love." Um. Not. No way am I sitting here and typing in a whole three-page journal entry about Abuela. I flip around some more, skipping all the pages that I see Abuela's name written on. I stop on a page that has two words written at the top of it.

Spanish: Yo escribo
English: I write

Okay. Now this seems like it is worth typing out for translation. I position my water bottle on top of one side of the journal and my social studies book on the other to keep the journal from closing shut as I type Abuelo's words. When I finally finish typing everything on the page, I click Translate and sit back in my chair.

English: Words are important. They fly out of our mouths without much thought when we're mad. They slowly cruise from the depths of our core with much caution and preparation when sensitivity is needed. In joyous times, words continually flow from us with confidence and happiness.

However, what happens to the words we're afraid to let out? What happens to the words that we don't want to say to someone's face? What happens when words are all jumbled up in our throats, and we are unsure of how to get them out or what order to put them in to form a sentence?

Writing is important. Writing those words we don't know how to say out loud provides the ultimate satisfaction.

When I am confused about what to say, I write. I let the words splat on paper like globs of paint, running together to form the sentences my mouth can't or doesn't want to construct.

Then those words can breathe, live life. If I choose, I can share the paper that houses the words with people to read them and understand me. Or I can keep those pages to myself and be thankful the words no longer take up space in my mind.

Writing has been my form of therapy for many years

now. It helps me preserve the good memories and let go of the bad ones I caused or experienced. Writing is my outlet.

While I always knew Abuelo enjoyed writing, I never knew there was a specific reason for why he did it. Reading Abuelo's words has been like having a conversation with him, even though he's no longer here. It makes me feel all warm, like I'm wrapped up in my blanket fresh out of the dryer. I copy and paste the journal entry into a Word doc and save it on my desktop. I have a feeling I may want to reread it.

I lean back in my chair and look up at the ceiling. It's kind of cool that I've been using my journal the same way Abuelo used to use his. For him, writing was a way to express himself when he couldn't figure out what to say—sort of like what happened to me during my class presentation.

Wait a minute!

OMG!

I *know* I can do something like this for my magazine submission. But how?

Think, Sicily. Think.

How can I write about who I am and make it interesting enough for people to read? No one at my school would want to read about me. I'm not a DJ, like Ebony in the *Teen Vogue* article. I don't do anything cool like that.

I have to figure something out though; I'm running out

of time. The magazine submissions are due tomorrow. I look back at the computer screen. The section tabs at the top of the *Teen Vogue* site are the same as usual: Style, Politics, Culture, and Identity.

Culture.

Identity.

Culture.

Identity.

Something about these last two words stand out to me. Culture and identity have become so important these last couple of weeks, mostly because I had to do that presentation for Mrs. Taylor's class and because of all the questions I was asked.

I rest my head on my desk, next to my laptop.

Think, Sicily. Think.

I got it! Feeling like someone has flipped a switch on in my mind, I jump up from my chair.

Will it work?

My arms fly straight up into the air as if I'd just shot a three-pointer with seconds left on the clock. "Yes, it will work. I'm gonna do it," I shout. Finally, I have a topic. "I'm going to write about *this,* and it's going to be good."

TWENTY-NINE

≈≈≈

8:00 p.m.

7:12 A.M.

Fr: Marconi@Chisholm.edu

Bcc: SicilyJordan@eMail.com

Subject: Chisholm Is Talking—Submission Deadline Tonight at 8:00 p.m.

Hey all,

Today is the day. All magazine submissions are due by 8:00 p.m. tonight. Anything received after that will not be considered. You can reply to this email with your submission or stop by my class (Room 327) anytime today to drop it off.

As you all know, the magazine will be up and running this Friday. If you are chosen as a writer for the magazine, your submission will be posted on that day. If you do not get chosen, don't be discouraged. There will be other ways to contribute to the magazine throughout the school year.

Good luck!
Eric Marconi
Shirley Chisholm Middle School

Yes, 8:00 p.m.! If I come straight home from school, I should have plenty of time to write my submission before the deadline.

2:30 p.m.

I take my shoes off and sit on my bed with my laptop. I don't have time to waste, so handwriting a first draft is not an option. *BOING! BOING!* My phone is chiming, alerting me of text messages and DM notifications from the Tether Squad. I can't read any of them now. I have to focus.

5:00 p.m.

It took longer than I expected, but I finally finished my draft. Instead of sending it to Mr. Marconi, I'll let it sit for a minute and take a break because I'm starving. I haven't eaten anything since lunch. When I open my bedroom door, the smell of fried chicken fills my room, and my stomach starts dancing.

In the kitchen, Pa is standing over the FryDaddy, waiting to take cooked pieces of chicken out.

"Where's Ma?" I ask.

"She has to stay late at the bank tonight for a meeting, so I'm in charge of dinner. We are having fried chicken and fries."

"Don't forget to say grace over the food," I tell him, giggling. "I'm reminding you since Ma's not here."

"I know, I know," he says.

"Hola, mi amor."

I spin around and see Abuela walking into the kitchen. *Ugh*, she's probably here because Ma is still at work. I give her a half smile, half smirk, and turn away from her. Just because she sat and watched me try to braid my hair the other day without saying anything mean doesn't make us cool.

Enrique comes into the kitchen, hugs Abuela, and sits next to her. *Traitor.* I roll my eyes at him and take out three plates from the cabinet. I toss one down on the table to Enrique and place one at Pa's and my seats.

"¿Dónde está mi plato?" Abuela asks. Even though I understand what she means, I ignore her. Pa gets a plate for her and brings it over with a large pan of chicken strips and fries. Since he doesn't say anything about me not giving Abuela a plate, I decide to go easy on her tonight. But if she starts with me, that will go right out the window.

"This is dinner?" Abuela asks.

"Sí, this is dinner, Mamá."

"Hey Pa, I've been working on my magazine submission all afternoon. Can you edit it for me?"

"All afternoon?" Pa says. "You know the rules around here. Homework first. That's the priority. This magazine thing is not something you should have been working on all afternoon."

"¿Qué magazine?" Abuela asks, winking at me.

"It's something for school," I say through my teeth.

When Abuela opens her mouth to say something else, I cut her off.

"I don't have any homework," I lie.

Mrs. Taylor assigned another historical timeline for us to fill in, and it's due tomorrow. But I'm so close to being done with my submission that I can't stop now. Homework will have to wait till later or might not even get done at all.

"If she's doesn't have any homework, what's the problem?" Abuela says, wiping her mouth. "Let her work on the magazine. It *is* school-related."

Now this. This is my abuela. Even though I'm glad this version of her—the version I used to know—has creeped out and joined us for dinner, I'm not falling for it. After seeing the wink she gave me when she cut Pa off right as he was about to lecture me about priorities, I get what's she doing. It's why she sat and watched me try to braid my hair the other day. Abuela wants back in. It's not happening.

"Fine, Sicily," Pa says. "I'll review your submission."

"Thanks, Pa." I shove a handful of fries into my mouth as I get up from the table and say, "I'm going to go finish it. I'll come back later to clean up," before running up to my room.

5:45 p.m.

I grab my phone and look through all the alerts and text notifications. I have five messages, all from Michael. He's sent some pictures of Reyna and me and a few of just me.

Sicily Jordan

These look good! Thanx 4 sending. When did u take them????

Michael Sado

Yesterday when u and Reyna were sitting on the driveway. I took them b4 u guys noticed me. I thought u might want them.

You look really pretty.

My cheeks tickle a little as I reread that last message.

Thanx. I think I might use 1 of them for my magazine submission.

Cool, did u turn it in yet?

Shoot! My submission. I need to finish it. I send a quick message to Michael telling him I will text him later. I take my laptop over to my desk and spend the next hour revising and editing. The time I spent away from my draft was good because I can now see where things need to be moved around or written differently.

7:10 p.m.

I print my submission in Pa's office.

"Pa! Where are you?" I shout.

"In the living room with Abuela."

Great, she's still here.

In the living room, Pa is leaning all the way back in the recliner, watching the news. Abuela is sitting on the couch, drinking something thick and brownish, probably for her arthritis pain.

"Here it is, Pa," I say, handing him my submission and a pen.

He starts reading it while I stand next to him, and I feel

Abuela's eyes on me. I want to ask her what she's looking at. I know better, so I keep my mouth shut.

"I forgot I need to clean the kitchen. Pa, let me know when you're done." Since Ma's still at work, it would have been easy to skip out on cleaning up tonight, but I'll do anything to get away from Abuela.

7:20 p.m.

"Here you go. Good job. Just make these few changes," Pa says. I flick soap bubbles off my hands over the sink and stand next to him, so I can see what he is talking about. The paper has a few markings he made with the red pen.

"Thanks!"

In my room, I make the changes Pa noted, format the document, and draft my email. I have no idea how Mr. Marconi will feel about my submission or if he'll even understand what I'm talking about. But this topic is important to me. If I get picked to write for the magazine, hopefully, I'll be able to write more on this subject.

7:52 p.m.

Fr: SicilyJordan@eMail.com
To: Marconi@Chisholm.edu
Subject: Chisholm Is Talking—Submission

Hi Mr. Marconi,

My submission and a photo for the online magazine are attached.

Thanks!
Sicily Jordan

I say a quick prayer and click Send. Once the email disappears from my screen, I feel like "Sicily is a writer" has been written in cement.

I love that writing in my journal has not only helped me get back into writing and learning about where I come from but has also helped me piece together my draft. Instead of being so focused on Erin Masterson, wondering if I'll get picked for the magazine, and everything else, I should have just sat with my paper, pen, and thoughts. If I had, I bet I would have been able to finish this submission a long time ago. I have to remember not to do things just to prove myself to others. The only person I need to prove something to is myself.

8:30 p.m.

I've looked at the pictures Michael sent over a hundred times. My favorite is the one with Reyna and me laughing.

Reyna is holding her stomach and looking up at the sky, with her mouth wide open. My eyes are closed tight, and I'm smiling.

I crop the picture a little and play around with different filters. When I find one I like, I post the photo and type in a caption:

StylishSicilyJ

> Crackin up with my girl @QueenReyna!
> Photo: @YaBoyM.Sado

Before I can even put my phone down, there are forty likes on the picture, and Evelyn has commented:

EvTheDiva

> I went to the page of the boy who took this pic.
> HE IS CUTE!!!!

And the rest of the Tether Squad follows up with:

itsSamaraMara

> You have the best smile! Who's that boy???

Lexi 🖤

> 👆 Same comment. SAME QUESTION! 👆

THIRTY

Te Amo, Sicily

"WANNA GO TO the gas station and get Slurpees?" Reyna asks.

"Yeah, let's see if Kamaya and Kiara wanna go."

Reyna and I walk down the ramp from our classroom to the courtyard.

When we get to our bench, Kamaya is already there, scrolling through her phone.

"Hey, girl. We're going to get Slurpees. Wanna come?" I ask her.

"Yes, I *need* one. Mrs. Wilson is crazy. She just gave us a bunch of homework, and it's all due tomorrow. Tonight is TGIT! Thursday night TV is the best. You guys are lucky you don't have her."

"Well, at least tomorrow is Friday," Reyna says, trying

to cheer her up. Kamaya covers her face with her hands and pretends to cry.

"Where is Kiara?" I ask.

"Oh, she went home early, like an hour after lunch. So let's go!" Kamaya says, standing up.

When we near the gate to exit campus, I see Michael walking with a group of boys. He gives me a head nod, and I wave as he walks over to us.

"There's your bae," Reyna says.

"What? Whose bae? Where?" Kamaya asks, looking around.

I give Reyna a look that says, *Chill out*. She shrugs and smiles.

"Wassup, y'all?" Michael says to us.

"Hi," Kamaya says, smiling and giggling.

"See you tomorrow," Reyna says. She pulls Kamaya's arm and locks hers around it. "Let's let them hang out," I hear her tell Kamaya.

"Why are they acting weird?" Michael asks.

"I don't know. I thought we were going to get Slurpees."

"I was gonna ask if I could walk you home, but if you wanna go catch up with them—"

"NO! I mean. I can go with them tomorrow. So, we can walk. Um, I mean, you can walk with me if you want to."

"Cool. Let's go."

Unlike the other day at Reyna's house, there is no weird silence between us. As we walk, Michael and I talk about our day at school, plans for the weekend, and how I feel about the magazine writers being announced tomorrow.

"I can always try again next year," I tell him.

"It sounds like you think you're not gonna get picked."

"I'm just not sure."

"I think you'll get picked," he says, reaching for my hand. I look down at his fingers interlocked with mine. I now understand what it means when people say they have butterflies in their stomach.

Michael's hand is warm and soft, just like it was when he helped me up after knocking me down at Reyna's house. Wow, look how far we have come since then. Wait, what if Pa comes home early from work again? The butterflies in my stomach land, and I loosen my grip on his hand.

Then Michael squeezes a little, and I no longer care who might see us. I even start walking slower so I can have more time with him. My phone rings in my back pocket, and I leave it there. Nothing is going to interrupt this moment.

"What ever happened with your dress?" Michael asks. "Did you get it cleaned?"

I lower my head. "My pollera? No, I'm scared it might rip in the washing machine, and I don't have enough money to dry clean it. I haven't figured out any other way to get it cleaned."

"Maybe you should tell your parents what happened. They might understand that it was just an accident."

Even though I've thought a lot about coming clean to Ma, I turn and look at Michael as if his head just exploded. He faces forward, and neither of us says a word.

We turn the corner onto Castle Lane, and I see my house. There are no cars in the driveway. *Yes.* No parents. Hopefully, Enrique isn't home either.

"Welp, this is my house," I say when we arrive. We stop walking and stand facing each other on the sidewalk, still holding hands. Branches and leaves from the big tree in my front yard sway in the wind above us.

"Thanks for walking me home." I hold his hand tighter. I don't want to let go, but there is no way I can invite him in. I'm not allowed to have anyone over without permission from Ma or Pa first.

"I have to get to practice." Michael pulls me into him. As if already trained for this moment, my arms slide around his neck, his around my waist. My body tightens as I imagine Enrique watching us from his bedroom window.

Relax, Sicily. Breathe, Sicily.

I rest my head on his shoulder, and I close my eyes. It feels like we're floating.

"I'll text you later," he whispers into my ear. We both let go of each other, and neither of us moves. My mind is telling me to go inside. My heart says to stay right here. And my feet, they're confused. Michael takes a step forward, and just when I think he's about to hug me again, he kisses my cheek. My heart starts beating fast like it's going to jump right out of my chest.

"Bye," he says, walking away. I turn and watch him until he reaches the corner.

Everything has changed. Is Michael my boyfriend now? Will we hold hands at school like other couples do? Do we need to post selfies of each other on our pages to make *us* official? My neighbor's dog starts barking from behind their fence, and I snap back into reality. *Chill, Sicily. Don't start acting boy-crazy like Evelyn.*

I walk up to my front door, stick my key in, and unlock the door with one hand. My other hand is busy cupping my cheek where Michael just kissed it. Inside, I lean my back up against the door and close my eyes.

"Hola, mi amor," I hear from the living room.

I open my eyes slowly and remove my hand from my cheek. Pa's not home, so why is Abuela here? Honestly, who cares? I'm not about to let her ruin my good mood. She starts saying something from where she is in the living room. I just ignore her and head up to my room.

At the top of the stairs, I hear Abuela say *pollera*, and I stop. *Did she find it?*

My mouth becomes dry. I want to ask her to repeat what she said, but a part of me knows I don't need to. Trouble is coming my way. I go straight to Enrique's room and open his door just in time to hear Kendrick Lamar telling me to "be humble, sit down." I press pause on his portable speaker.

"Hey! What are you doing?" Enrique shouts. He is sitting in his gamer chair in front of the TV with a controller in his hand.

"Why is Abuela here?"

"Ma told me to tell you to give Abuela your pollera. Something about them letting someone borrow it."

"What! Who? Why?"

"I don't know. Ma said she called you. Maybe you should have answered and asked *her* all these questions yourself."

My eyes fill with tears, and I walk out of his room.

"Today is the day Ma kills me," I whisper.

In my room, I slide the closet door open and take out my laundry basket. I dig through the basket and pull out my pollera. *Yuck!* It smells like a gross mixture of sweat and Febreze. I spread my pollera out on my bed, drop to my knees, and cover my face.

The stain has not disappeared like I prayed so many times for it to do. Tears rush down my face. And then I hear a light tapping on my door. I grab a dirty shirt from the floor and blow my nose. Before I can say anything, Abuela opens the door and looks in. When she sees my face, she pushes the door all the way open and rushes to my side.

"Look." I point at my pollera. "I ruined it."

"Cálmate." Abuela rubs my back as more tears flow.

"Ma is going to kill me. She told me not to take it out of the plastic garment bag, and I didn't listen to her."

"Don't worry." Abuela runs her stiff bent fingers back and forth over the stain, then picks up my pollera. Her jaw gets tight as she stares at her hands. I stare at them too, as they struggle to fold the pollera. Abuela grabs my overnight bag from the corner and pushes my pollera inside, all while making a face that tells me she is in pain.

"Shhh," she says, with her crooked index finger over her mouth. "I will clean it."

Is she serious? Maybe she's doing it so she can have something over Ma. Or maybe this is her way of making things right between us. I rub my wet eyes and look at her standing near my door now with the bag strap over her shoulder.

She looks like she wants to say something, and I know I *need* to say something before she leaves. When I try to, the words become stuck, like peanut butter on the roof of my mouth.

"Did you finish that magazine thing yesterday?" Abuela asks, not looking directly at me.

"Um, yeah." I blow my nose again, then add, "I saw how you got Pa off my back about doing homework first. Thanks."

Abuela gives me a small smile and continues standing there quietly. My heart pounds. *I hope she doesn't say anything to ruin this moment.*

She walks back over to where I am, still on my knees, and sits on my bed, placing the bag on her lap. "You know, I had a talk with your Pa the other day."

"You did?" I ask, acting surprised.

"Yes, he helped me realize I need to change my old ways of thinking." She looks in my eyes and continues. "He reminded me that words have the power to help or destroy."

I look down and pick at my nail polish, then I smile, thinking back to when I heard Pa say that to her. That night, I thought their conversation was pointless and that Abuela would never change. I guess she just needed some time.

"I miss how we used to be," she says.

I nod in agreement.

"It's only been a few weeks. Still, I feel like I've missed so much. The last time we had a real conversation, you were nervous about not having friends at your new school. I have no idea how your first day was, if you have friends now, and I still don't fully understand this magazine thing you're doing."

Abuela is right; so much has happened in a short amount of time. If we'd been cool, Abuela would know about everything going on with me—even about the kiss I just got from Michael.

"You know, I was ready to cut you off forever," I say. "Treat you like a stranger, like you never existed."

Abuela puts her hand to her chest and in a flat voice says, "I noticed." She then stands with the bag and walks to the door. "I hope you and I can be close again. I don't want to miss out on anything going on in your life."

Even though everything Abuela is saying is nice and sweet, I can't help feeling like we talked *around* the problem and solved nothing. I have to tell her how I feel about what she said to me, just like how I told Pa how I felt about him not standing up for me to her.

I can't let her slide. She really hurt me.

Before Abuela closes my bedroom door behind her, I clear my throat, stand up, and take Ma's advice to talk to Abuela about how I feel.

"Abuela, why don't you like my hair?" I ask.

"What?" Abuela comes back into my room and stares at me. I can tell by the look on her face that she is trying to figure out an answer, but I keep going.

"I love my hair. I can do so many different things to it. I can wear braids or flat twists, straighten it, or go with my natural tight curls. My hair is beautiful in any style." Words keep flying out of my mouth as fast as I can think of them. "You hurt me a lot when you said I look ghetto and low-class."

Abuela stands there, just staring with glossy, wet eyes.

"Just because my hairstyles are different from what you are used to doesn't mean I have bad hair."

I can no longer read the look on Abuela's face. If she's mad and changes her mind about cleaning my pollera, it doesn't matter. I'm good now. I feel so much better after telling her

271

how I feel. It's like I'm suddenly free from the ten pounds of emotions that have been chained to me for the last few weeks.

Abuela comes over to me, stretches her arm up, and puts her hand on my head. She moves her hand down my French braid and to my back. "I think you are beautiful," she says. "I was wrong to say those things about you and your hair. Lo siento," Abuela apologizes.

Like some kind of switch, those two words release all the pain and anger I've been holding in. I wrap my arms around her shoulders and squeeze gently.

"I'll never speak to you like that again." She tilts my head down, kisses my forehead, and then walks to the door again.

"Oh, and you should stop drinking castor oil for your arthritis pain. I read that it's like a laxative," I say, making the puke green emoji face. "Rubbing it into your skin like lotion is way better."

She smiles. "Te amo, Sicily," she says and closes my door behind her.

THIRTY-ONE

They Actually Understand

MA SLEPT IN today, so Pa drops me off at school earlier than usual. None of my friends are at our bench in the courtyard yet, so I pull out my phone and check my email again. Still nothing from Mr. Marconi. I go to the school magazine website. Nothing there either. Just the same countdown clock I saw earlier this morning with a note that says the site will be live at 1:00 p.m., which is right after lunch when I'm already back in class and not allowed to use my phone. Mr. Marconi should have emailed the writers he picked.

There's no use in refreshing the page so I go to the bathroom to check myself out and kill some time. When I push the door open, the smell of Listerine surrounds me. Erin Masterson turns from the bathroom sink with a small bottle of it in her hand. She is wearing a pin that says, *Smile, It's Good for You*. That must not apply to her because she's frowning.

I've seen her around school and during lunch the last couple of days. This is the first time we've been near each other since what happened online the other day. I walk past her and don't bother looking in her direction. At the full-length mirror on the other side of the bathroom, I take out my lip gloss and dab some onto my lips. In the mirror's reflection, I watch her, just in case. Her face looks like she just sucked on a lemon or something gross as she types into her phone.

She looks over at me, and I'm ready if she says or tries anything. But I guess she knows better because she flips her hair over her shoulder and leaves. I roll my eyes as the bathroom door slams shut. She's not so tough without her two bodyguards. That girl is all talk, and I'm glad I sent in a magazine submission. After leaving the bathroom, I don't see Erin Masterson for the rest of the day. Not even during lunch like I usually do.

When the bell rings, everyone takes their sweet time getting up from the lunch tables, except me. I want to sprint back to class to see if I can get on the computer and check the school's magazine site.

"Hey, good luck," Michael says, high-fiving me. He didn't sit with me at lunch, hold my hand, or mention anything about being my boyfriend, and I'm okay with all of that. I like things just the way they are with us. For now.

We interlock our fingers after our palms connect. And then he smiles at me. All I can hear and feel are exploding fireworks, like some kind of celebration that's only for Michael and me, just because we're touching.

"Thanks, seriously," I say to him, and Reyna and I head off to our class.

"Ugh, you two." Reyna laughs. "Anyway, I can't wait to see the magazine. Last night, Michael and I were getting along for like two seconds, and he showed me some of the pictures he took for other people's submissions," Reyna says as we walk. "Some of their topics are really cool. I wish you would tell me what you ended up writing about."

"You'll have to wait and see," I say with a smile. A second later, my knees start feeling weak, like they will bend and I'll collapse right here in front of everyone. I told Reyna she'd have to wait and see, but what if Mr. Marconi didn't pick me? I slow down, and Reyna looks at me. I hold on to her arm and smile, so she doesn't ask me what's wrong.

In class, I slide down into my desk. The cold plastic chair cools my hot body as I take a few breaths. What if Erin Masterson was right? What if she was so quiet in the bathroom this morning because she already knew I didn't get picked? She probably didn't think she needed to rub it in before I got the chance to click through the magazine for myself to see that my submission was not posted.

"Class," Mrs. Taylor says, getting our attention. "I'm not sure if you heard that our school's online magazine launched today."

I pop my head up and stare at Mrs. Taylor. "Here it is," she says, pointing to the SMART Board screen.

I'm shocked at how nice it looks. Whoever designed the site did a good job. The home page has a crisp white background with *Chisholm Is Talking* in a big, bold font at the top. Even though the words are a hideous mix of our blue and orange school colors, the words pop out nicely against the white.

Above the title, in the right corner, are all the links for the school's social media pages, and in the middle of the page is a photo slideshow. Each photo has a title above it, which I assume are the selected writers' submissions.

I sit up straight in my seat and lean forward a little. Rubbing my moist hands together, I look at Reyna.

"This is it!" she whispers.

I stare at the slideshow, and I pray the photo I sent in with my submission appears. Just as the second picture is about to flip to the third, Mrs. Taylor clicks on it, stopping the images from moving. She starts talking to the class about the magazine's purpose and why it's so important to the school. She then clicks one of the tabs in the drop-down menu at the top of the page and reads the welcome message posted on the first page. She also reads all the information on the other three tabs too.

What is she doing? I rest my elbows on my desk and hold my head up with my fists. Why is she dragging this out?

Blah, Blah, Blah! She keeps reading and reading, and I want to scream.

"So I want to go back to the first page and show you all something," Mrs. Taylor says. "In this photo slideshow are the articles written by students selected to write for the magazine this year. I was told that over twenty-five students submitted an article or a story, and only ten were chosen. I am pleased to announce that someone in this class was picked!" Mrs. Taylor finally clicks the slideshow, allowing it to play.

IT'S ME! There I am!

The picture Michael took of me sitting on Reyna's driveway is smack in the center of the screen for everyone to see.

Reyna turns to me with the biggest smile. "Congrats, bestie!" she says.

"Sicily wrote a wonderful piece for the magazine, and I want her to come up and read it." Mrs. Taylor turns to me. "Will you, Sicily? I can read it, but I think it would be better if you did."

My pulse starts racing, and I feel light-headed. I can't believe it. I *actually* got picked.

"Here is her submission." Mrs. Taylor clicks on the title above my picture, and a new page opens. My picture is now at the top, followed by my words.

"Wow, Sicily. You look pretty in that picture," Allen says.

"Thanks." Michael captured a great moment. My face is tilted up a little and has a hint of a smile.

"Yay!" Reyna screams as I get up from my desk. As I walk to the front of the room, the class starts clapping for me. I can't believe this is happening. Mrs. Taylor hands me a printed copy of my submission, and I turn and face everyone. Before I begin reading, I take a quick look down at the anklet Abuela gave me. I put it on for the first time this morning hoping it would bring me luck, and it did.

"After my presentation a few weeks ago, a lot of you were confused about me being Black and my family being from Panamá," I say. "I wrote this to clear some things up for you and also for myself." I take a deep breath and start reading from the paper.

Black and Panamanian. No, Black Panamanian.

I understand this is new and different for many people, and it is okay to ask questions if you don't understand. What is not okay is telling a Black person (or any person) they are lying because you don't understand the difference between race and culture.

Let me explain.

I come from a long line of Black men and women whose skin ranges from the lightest color of sand to the darkest shade of chocolate. I come from a line of people who can be traced from Panamá to the Caribbean and then to Africa.

I come from parents who were born in Panamá. A country where the strength and courage of Bayano, an escaped slave, still fills its people with pride.

I come from a line of men who, despite being discriminated against, faced dangerous conditions and helped build one of the Seven Wonders of the Modern World, the Panamá Canal.

I come from a line of women who passed down the technical skills of hair braiding. Just as they did a long time ago, I proudly wear my hair in braids too. The detail of their braid designs spoke of the tribes the women belonged to and displayed the beauty and creativity of who they were. And to this day, that same beauty has set trends that the world tries to copy. The line I come from weaves through different countries and cultures and makes me who I am.

When people ask, "What are you?" I proudly respond, "I am Afro-Panamanian. I am a Black Panamanian."

Afro (short for *African*) comes before Panamanian to let people know I am of African ancestry. And because I am a direct descendant of people from a Latin American country, I am Latina. Panamanian or Latina, either way, I am always Afro and Black first.

No matter the shade of our skin, Black people everywhere belong to the same race. Regardless of our culture, our differences are to be respected. None of us fits perfectly into a box. Many things define and make us who we are.

My Black skin does not make me less Panamanian. And being Panamanian adds to but takes nothing away from what the color of my skin represents.

Still staring at my words on the page, I feel brave and strong, like a new and improved Sicily. This is a huge difference from the last time I stood in front of my class. I no longer have to worry about what happened then, because today has filled me with a glow that's shining within me right now.

"Great job, Sicily," Mrs. Taylor says. "And you are right. Culture and race are two different things. After reading this during lunch, I decided we will have a class discussion on race, ethnicity, and culture next week. I'm so glad you chose to write about this topic. And congratulations on being picked to write for the magazine. I see a great future for you as a writer."

Even though I would rather hear that from my parents, it's just as important that Mrs. Taylor notices my talent.

"How come we don't hear much about Black people like you?" Aaron asks.

"Because Black people, no matter their cultural background, are hardly ever given the same opportunities as those who aren't Black," I say. "And because of that, you all think people from Latin American countries are white. Then you see someone like me and think I'm lying because I don't look like what you are used to seeing. People like me are finally starting to get the attention we deserve. It doesn't seem like it's happening fast enough though."

It is so much easier to have this conversation now and answer their questions this time. What a difference it makes to be able to speak about myself confidently.

"I have a question," James says. "Instead of coming here, Black people from Africa decided to go to Panama, is that right?"

"Well, kind of," I say. "Some made a choice." I pause and wait till everyone is looking at me. "Many Black people were forced to go to Panamá and other countries. There's this whole thing called the slave trade. Maybe Mrs. Taylor can talk about that next week too."

I walk back to my desk with my head up high. *They get it. They actually understand.*

"I never knew about any of this," I hear someone say.

Without looking around to see who said it, I pull out my

journal from my bag and slip the printed copy of my magazine article into the middle of it.

I close my eyes and whisper, "Gracias, Abuelo. Thank you for the gift."

~~~~~~~~~~~~~~~~~~~~~~~~~~~~~~~~~~~~~~~

Dear Journal,

Today's fact: I don't have one. But today was perfect, so I figured I'd write about it instead.

You-know-who walked me home again and invited me to his basketball game at the park tomorrow afternoon. I have to be careful what I write about that person in here, just in case someone reads this. . . .

The magazine!!!! I'm so glad all the stress is behind me. When I got home from school, I clicked through the articles and didn't see anything written by Erin Masterson or any of her friends. And there was no fashion section either. I wish I could have seen her salty face when she saw my submission was posted.

After dinner, I showed my family the online magazine and read my article for them. Ma and Pa told me they were proud of me and said how impressed they were with my writing. They told me to keep practicing because writing could open doors for me in the future. So it sounds kind of like maybe they are changing their minds about writing being more than a hobby. Even Enrique had something nice to say before he left to meet his friends.

The shocker was Abuela. Tears dropped from her eyes as she went on and on about how my writing reminded her of Abuelo's. She got up from the couch and shouted, "I knew it! I knew you had the gift!"

I'm so glad she is back to being the Abuela I used to have fun with, because I missed her.

After going through all of this, I now understand what Mrs. Taylor meant on the first day of school when she said we'd be a part of growth and change at Shirley Chisholm Middle School.

I hope to continue being a part of that growth and change by telling more of my people's stories.

Sincerely,
Sicily

llllllllllllllllllllll

SICILY'S GLOSSARY OF ALL THINGS SPANISH AND PANAMANIAN

~~~~~~~~~~~~~~~~~~~~~~~~~~~~~~~~~~~~~~~

arroz con pollo [a-rros kon po-io]

noun

1. rice and chicken cooked together in one big pot
2. a dish Ma makes at least once a month

bata [baa-tuh]

noun

1. a house dress
2. a dress Ma wears around the house to clean and sleep in

cálmate [kahl-mah-te]

verb

1. calm down
2. what Ma and Pa will say to me when I'm talking too fast or doing too much

carimañola [ka-ri-ma-nyo-la]

noun

1. meat stuffed in yucca, then fried
2. a dish Panamanians eat at parties

delicioso [de-li-sio-so]

adjective

1. delicious
2. what I say whenever I eat Red Vines and yummy pizza

empanadas [em-pa-na-das]

noun

1. dough filled with meat, then baked (I don't like them fried)

ensalada de papa [en-sa-la-da de pa-pa]

noun

1. potato salad
2. a dish I only eat when Ma makes it

excelente [eks-se-len-te]

adjective

1. excellent
2. what Ma and Pa always say to me (but not Enrique) when they see my report card

hojaldras [o-hal-dras]

noun

1. fried bread
2. a dish Pa makes on Saturday mornings (I like to put butter and cheese on mine)

Nochebuena [no-che-bue-na]

noun

1. the Good Night
2. Christmas Eve, when my whole family gets together to eat a lot of food, dance, and stay up all night

novellas [no-be-las]

noun

1. soap operas
2. dramatic TV shows that come on in the middle of the day on the Spanish channel

quinceañera [kin-se-a-nye-ra]

noun

1. a big party to celebrate when a girl turns fifteen and becomes a woman, according to Ma

reggae en Español [re-gei en-spuhn-yowl]

noun

1. reggae in Spanish
2. traditional Jamaican reggae with lyrics in Spanish

reggaetón [re-ge'ton]

noun

1. a music style from Puerto Rico that was influenced by reggae en Español from Panamá

sancocho [san-ko-cho]

noun

1. a yummy soup with potatoes, meat, veggies, and other stuff

soca [so-ka]

noun

1. music influenced by African (of course) and East Indian rhythms

sorrel [sor-ruhl]

noun

1. a purplish drink made with stuff that tastes bitter, so you have to add a lot of sugar to it (a bunch of people love it, but I don't)

tontería [ton-te-ri-a]

noun

1. foolishness
2. what Pa calls the music and TV shows that Enrique and I love

AUTHOR'S NOTE

Dear Reader,

Sincerely Sicily is loosely based on my experiences growing up and came out of a need for representation and understanding. As a child, I didn't fully comprehend how to explain my Black Panamanian background when people asked, "What are you?"

Being asked that question, coupled with the fact that I was growing up in a predominantly white community as a Black Latina, I often felt out of place. My peers were all the same, and not only was I of a different race, but my culture was something that was entirely out of their realm of understanding.

I always wished for a point of reference, someone I could point to and say, "I'm just like them." But characters in books, movies, and TV shows didn't look like me, nor did their experiences resemble mine.

As I got older, I realized people wanted to put me in a box based on either my race or my culture. There was never a place for me to exist as I am fully. It was either Black or

Latina (never both). And because I visually present as the Black woman I am, my Latina culture was always met with skepticism.

Writing *Sincerely Sicily* was very liberating, as it allowed me to thoroughly share my Black Panamanian background in a way I have never been able to do before. I have so many hopes for this book, but the main one is that when readers finish, they walk away from it with a clear understanding of the African diaspora, which is vast and spans worldwide.

Sincerely,
Tamika Burgess

ACKNOWLEDGMENTS

Thank you first and always to my Lord, Jesus Christ. I started the first version of this book in 2013, and here it is, finally out in the world in 2023. Without God's direction, grace, and favor, I would never have remained dedicated throughout ten years of writing, rewriting, revising, and editing.

"But as for you, be strong and do not give up, for your work will be rewarded" (2 Chron. 15:7).

Thank you to my agent, Regina Brooks, and the Serendipity Literary Agency team. Regina, you believed in this story from the first time you read it, and that gave me the push to press on as we went through revision after revision after revision, LOL! I am so grateful for the wealth of knowledge you have shared with me.

To everyone at HarperCollins who had a role in bringing *Sincerely Sicily* into the world, thank you! Specifically to my editor, Carolina Ortiz. From our first conversation, I loved your enthusiasm for the story, and I knew it would be in good hands with you. I genuinely appreciate you tending to all my questions and concerns; your diligence and thoughtfulness during this process will never be forgotten.

To music historian Katelina "Gata" Eccleston, thank you for helping me get the historical Panamanian reggaeton information right. And to Professor Melva Lowe de Goodin, thank you for reading the entire story and making sure dates, names, places, etc., were all correct. I am so thankful to you both for helping me accurately share *our* Panamanian history.

To my "author friends": Elizabeth Acevedo, Alaya Dawn Johnson, and Natalia Sylvester, thank you for responding to my emails, candidly answering all my questions, and sharing your experiences as authors with me. Having you three to reach out to has made everything less scary.

To anyone who ever read early versions of Sicily's story and anyone who answered questions to help me shape the characters, thank you for your help. Special shout-out to my NYC writing group: Jovie Last, David Quiles Guzman, and Christina Ramos Palau. I will never forget our monthly meetings at Panera Bread in Union Square. You all really stuck it out with me, chapter by chapter. I share this win with the three of you. ☺

To content editor Eileen Robinson, thank you also for helping me shape the early version of this story. Your feedback helped me get the story to a place where I felt comfortable enough to submit it to an agent.

To Marcela Landres and the Comadres and Compadres Writers Conference. It was at the first-ever conference in Brooklyn that I decided to move forward with writing a book. Marcela, thank you for being a reliable resource over the years and for connecting me with Eileen.

To my extended family, thank you all for the endless support. To my friend Tatiana Espy, you were there from the beginning when we were running around NYC and I was constantly telling you I was writing a book. Your continued support means everything to me! To my cousin Kilsha Castro, thank you for always believing in and supporting literally everything I do. To my Tía Mirta, thank you for calling and encouraging me to keep going with this story when I had put it down and thought I couldn't go any further with it. Thank you for sharing what the Lord told you to tell me about taking my book to the next level. To my Tía Mercedes, thank you for always being your fabulous self. Tía Fina in this story is you!

To my dad and brother, Guillermo Sr. and Jr., you both were the inspirations for the father and son in this story. Thanks for letting me use your middle name for those characters. Guillermo Jr., thanks for printing out many of my revised drafts. You saved me lots of $$$. Romina, Guillermo III, and Gianna, thank you for cheerleading from the sidelines and voting on things when I couldn't make decisions throughout this process.

And to my mom, Yolanda, thank you for letting me pick

your brain about all things Panamá, for calling friends and family to gather information for me, and for letting me talk your ear off when I was pondering ideas. Most importantly, thank you for simply being there for me, always.

To my beautiful Black Panamanians, this book is for us! We don't often get to read about our culture in fiction books, so I am happy and honored to share our history with the world.

And last but not least, in any way, to you, the reader. Thank you! I hope this story resonates with you regardless of gender, age, race, or cultural background.

"The idea is to write it so that people hear it and
it slides through the brain and goes straight to the heart."
—Maya Angelou